HORSE LEAD TO WATER

ADAM T. BROWN

Adam T. Brown Publish

For Information about this title or to order other books and/or
electronic media,
make all inquiries to:

Adam T. Brown
EmailsForAdam@tbrownwriting.com
tbrownwriting.com.

:ISBN 978-1-7343549-1-1 (paperback)

Library of Congress Control Number: 2019919677

Cover and Interior design: Adam T. Brown

First Edition

Chapters:

①

Enjoying the game of picking straws. One of the simpler
ways to greatly favor risk over reward. The shortest straw
claims the drawn as one of it's own. Delighted in being the
figurehead for the band of losers, it spends almost no time on
the sidelines and jumps immediately back into the fold.
When it reappears, it's initial blow is softened by the high
stakes endorphin. Should the straws be plucked from a
partial hand and the foul isn't seen, the person exempt from
the drawing wins. It is not a pretty victory and usually is
retribution for past defeats, from those who now were none
the wiser. Pettiness has no place in the world of favors, but is
front and center in the words of strangers.

For those who find themselves in unenviable positions.
Don't. You can dig your job like a grave or hate that you
need to be paid, but the results seldom change. There is a
feeling that things are going pretty good, but perhaps are
worse, or that somewhere the long straw lifer's are
prospering. Try to stay at a happy medium. Throw blame
when needed and pity parties when called for.

When playing a game it is important that the rules are
followed. Without rules there is no game and it's just,
everyday, life. There are rules that guide lives but were
mostly put in place so that individuals would not. Conversely,
one cannot be an individual if the loosely agreed upon
structure is followed. Since life is not a game or is yet to
defined, how any lives move forward drudges up the mind.
Judge anyone that thoughts could be had about for thinking
themself better or lesser.

It would have felt like winter just ended had it not been for the vengeful ice being spit at the face. It was late autumn and the rescue apples around the trees looked up pleadingly. They weren't given the time of day, for fear they would realize how late in the season it was. Nor were their spirits crushed or the soft exterior that housed them. A bushel of apples was from a nervous looking cashier whose bedside manner was lacking.

"You give them those years of life you've always heard you can never get back. And for what?" Was asked.

The cashier was paid. The dialogue could have been longer. No words were thought of that didn't lead to cliches, so no encouragement was given. The amount on the bill was declared instead.

It wasn't a nice day for anyone. Bubbly phrases that had been boiling over were recited to captive audiences of one. Dressed in a black robe and kneeling with an ear to the ground, a beggar tries to hear again. The beggar, sitting on their heels, is bent forward with their forehead to the ground. Apples are left for the beggar but they don't notice. Accustomed to hearing loose change hitting the fabric of the hat and pavement, they are unaware of the great gift that has been bestowed. These apples have come from an organic farm, which one can almost certainly feel good about. Continuing on, the panderer goes to a nearby coffee stop and pays with a card. As they're making their way back, they see the beggar. Face to the ground, though not as before. Now curled in a fetal position, some young kids are throwing the apples at the beggar. Since they were left, the apples had been sitting in the sun uncovered and had ripened. It only took a couple of rounds of throwing, watching the rebound and collecting the apples, before the children considered them broken.

Now before you say the panderer should have jumped in and stopped any madness, you must think of the children. Remember that they were standing directly over the beggar, and it doesn't take long to retrieve an apple that is right next to you. Travelling less and less the more it lost its shape. So by the time the panderer reached the beggar, not walking too fast for only a few sips of coffee had been had, the kids were gone. The panderer helped the beggar collect the coins scattered in bits of applesauce. The beggar was grateful for the help. The panderer didn't say it was they that had left the apples. If change were left maybe none of this would have happened. Or if something of the like had went down, perhaps the panderer would have been back sooner to help the beggar. Not having wasted precious seconds putting down the apples so they wouldn't bruise. Anyway, it wasn't just the beggar that apples were given to. By the time the panderer saw the beggar again, they were only holding their coffee and phone.

Recognize someone you don't know. They misread the recognition in the eyes, of knowing you don't know for something else, so they think they recognize you. So then you do think you know them, though now they are certain they don't know you. To walk up and talk would be rude for they appear to know you but you can't recall who they are, and want to respect this person who obviously seems to respect you.

On the topic of respect, which has to be considered an unalienable right, and one would not feel embarrassed if a right was violated but rather enraged, how can one person feel slighted by another and what is the correct course of action. If you go to shake someone's hand, in keeping up with traditions, and they make eye contact before looking at your hand and back to meet your gaze, without shaking your hand, your right to be respected has been violated. Depending on the person you may feel ashamed to have initiated the formality, or triviality, if the shake closed a deal. You may then be livid and in true fight or flight fashion, may attempt to grab at the withdrawn hand and lock on to the wrist accidentally.

Now you have violated the right of personal space. One affront is met by another. The scoreboard resets. The wrist is released and the physical assaulter is met by an emotional assailant. Accusations of amoral behavior are thrown at the hand shaker. No way to parry this verbal onslaught, not having a way with words and more known to talk with the hands. Both parties are eventually broken up, beaten down and struggling with themselves.

The troglodyte has respect for themself, the planet, and their neighbor. The troglodyte knows themself well enough to know that any reintroduction into society would only alienate them further from society. Since the troglodyte is already labeled as such, there can be no attempts to distance themself from that identity and rebrand. To be anything other than the troglodyte.

The troglodyte lived on the edge of town and would have never crossed anyone's radar had his definition for isolation changed. After thirty years of living in his controlled environment he decided to rejoin the living. Rifling through the closet he set his sights on what had been the latest fashion. He would appear as he had before, resurrecting the outfit. Wearing the clothes he was last seen in added to his mystique but was not his primary reason for choosing them. Instead, it was a subconscious fail-safe that would allow him to disintegrate should too much be asked of him socially.

He asked the stove that it not fail him now and cautiously turned a burner on. The stove complied and the troglodyte saw red before gaining his composure. He procured a non-perishable from the lazy Susan and a pot from above. In one swift movement he emptied the can with one hand and got the contents spinning with the other. Normally an extremely fast eater unconcerned with refining his taste, he took more time for this meal than usual. When he finally finished and had searched every inch of his bowl for anything more to eat, he noticed he had gotten something of a stain on his shirt. For the first time in a long time the troglodyte thought of a saying. They hadn't been much use to him of late and he saw them as commercially conversational, but one had him thinking. Who would advertise spilled milk? Either those people had their priorities wrong or were able to humiliate easily the hardened repressed.

The troglodyte left his humble home with thoughts of other things that needn't be cried. He hoped his arrival into town was one of them. He left without locking the front door and it wouldn't have done him any good if he had. The lock only worked to keep him in. He had it installed during his formative years, before his discipline had really developed. Even though he had chosen to live in isolation it was still good to know he could be forced to. He took a less than traveled path to town and had stopped bleeding by the time he had arrived. The bruises would come later.

When the troglodyte exited the wood he passed under the arches that shew the town's name for good luck. The arches were colored a soft blue so they would barely be noticeable. The town's name would be prominent instead. He walked the rest of the way into town on a path split down the middle. He stayed on the right side. It was after noon when his feet hit pavement.

The town looked very similar to the one he remembered. He wondered whether his memory was serving him or he his memory. He passed by a few people who were eager to start a conversation. Bereaved of the skill, it took him a couple of streets before he made a passing remark. After gaining some confidence in casual banter, he started inviting people to pay him a visit sometime. The troglodyte came from a time when people were constantly busy and dialogues would have to be paused. The first invitations were rejected. The troglodyte was too quick and what small talk had been established in no way encouraged invitees to find the troglodyte interesting. "But I don't even know you."

A young couple did take the troglodyte up on his offer. They met the troglodyte in front of a newsstand. He was busy looking up and down the street. They were busy-looking. They walked a little too quickly up to the troglodyte and asked him about his trouble. When the news seller returned and found the three of them playing door, plans were made that hopefully wouldn't go out the window.

The mark now on their calenders, the troglodyte and the couple parted. The troglodyte did a couple laps around his course but had no more successes. He was greeted with smiles though and worked on smiling back. The troglodyte knew the power of a smile but wasn't experiencing it's majesty in any of those interactions. After a while he chose not to smile back and continued to try to use words. The troglodyte was taking himself seriously and couldn't understand why other people were so afraid to do the same. A smile before acquaintances were made seemed like begging. A plea that no philosophic points be made. Not until one is better known should conversations be anything but vague and in no way heated. Knowing your own strength can have its disadvantages.

⑤

The troglodyte had developed a small following during his parading around. The office workers watching him couldn't see his expression from where they were, but knew it couldn't be a happy one. There were enough business folk watching to know that no one can handle that much rejection without those answers starting to be writ on their face. And what else could the troglodyte be doing but propositioning. There was no other reason for his dejected movements once his friends would leave him.

Office workers finished with their lunch would return to various floors and resume work. Hungry coworkers taking their spot. Once word had spread around the office, most of the building's residents took their lunch in the cafeteria so they could watch the troglodyte as well. A veteran with the company sent an intern down to scout. When the intern returned and told of the troglodyte's tactics, the higher up left their lunch unfinished to find superiors to complain to. Drawing customers away from the store front was a personal insult, even if the company was digitally based.

The cafeteria was on the fifth floor. The higher up conferred with their superiors on the third. He worked on the second, and the first floor was home to a half-library and other things being stored. The superiors gave the subordinate the time she needed to relay the story of the troglodyte, before assurances were given that the matter would be taken care of, and excused her with a new task. She was asked to compose an email for the town's council. She was told to sign for them. They would print out a copy to give of their voice.

...

The mid-level manager returned to her office to start the email. She had some experience writing to the council and a track record to prove it. Trying to correct any pitfalls of previous posts, she over thought and got no further than a subject line. Needing inspiration and a backstory for the troglodyte the council could believe, she closed the email and surfed the web. She contacted a few businesses, and, after selling them the idea of a bigger internet presence, contracted a few workers for a day job.

While the troglodyte was still in town, the blue collars went to his place and put signs around the property. The signs were not malicious or defamatory. Saying instead 'Keep Out' or 'Private Property'. The beware of dog signs returned with the contractors. With a perimeter of intent around the troglodyte's house, pedestrians would be dissuaded from visiting and the troglodyte would have one less reason to shame employee's work ethics while in town.

...

When the troglodyte stumbled out of the woods he saw the signs and immediately thought the worst. When he found his front door unlocked he let out a relief sigh and knew the house was still his. His next worry was about how he would be able to host people at his house if he sent mixed signals. He took the signposts out of the ground and turned them so the warning was faced towards the house. This was done so that his guests may feel welcome upon arrival. Possibly even cozy when they looked from the house to the woods.

The troglodyte had been lucky that day so knew worse things were set to happen. Seeing people again hadn't been how he thought it'd be and he wished to continue meeting them. He didn't want any more surprises at his house though, so he built a mailbox. The troglodyte would have access to the rest of the world without leaving his property. He would stay close to his house until the couple came, and after may have no reason to go back into town.

...

The mailbox needed a number, which meant the troglodyte needed an address. He used to pay taxes to the town and his house used to be listed. Some time during the troglodyte's absence from public service the town forgot about him. There were too many new housing developments to keep track of, and while some forests were cleared, the ones around the troglodyte continued to grow. When the house was no longer accessible by anything bigger than a dirt bike, one could question if there had ever been a house out there at all.

The troglodyte found the trail he took to town and started to break any branches that hadn't tried to break him, and were already broken. He didn't have a machete or anything like one, so he used his hands, knees, feet and occasionally forehead. He figured the path would need to be at least two people wide. He went with three to be safe. He cleared about a half mile before stopping for the night, giving him another four and a half to clear.

The troglodyte at night is as productive as during the day. Where other people might spend their free time leisurely, the unemployed troglodyte thinks up projects that will keep him occupied. His house being what it was, chores didn't take long. The troglodyte never made more work for himself, but was a perfectionist and redid chores during lapses of laziness. Otherwise he would often move things around, tinker with plastic or restructure his thoughts on past experiences.

To give him some semblance of time, he would leave a layout up in his house until something inspired him to change it. Counting sleep wasn't good for the troglodyte so he chose to wake up to the same scene every morning. The path clearing and journey to town was an event that reset his clock.

Curtains draped the refrigerator and two chairs were placed in front of it. His thinking was that if the curtains were left open, sun would shine on the fridge. Easier to cover the fridge so he wouldn't forget to shut the curtains. The chairs were for sitting and looking out the window, and getting only a tan if lucky. During this era there were instances when the troglodyte suffered mild heat stroke and dehydration. Trying to get bottles of water could prove difficult when the door handle was hotter than the curtains, which had been absorbing and transferring the heat. The troglodyte was never in very much trouble as quick relief was running alongside. Sometimes the situation was more dire, not checking that the fridge was stocked last time, reaches for a bottle that isn't there. He then peels out of the chair and makes his way to to the other side of the room to grab a spare case of water. He's better about having the cases stacked than fridge stocked. He brings the water back to the sitting chair and puts it on the one adjacent, before either grasping the handle through the curtain or handling the curtain to grasp the handle, and stocks the fridge. All water bottles go into the fridge, just as all water bottles go out. It would be less productive to take care of stocking the fridge during the night, when he could be more productive doing other things.

The troglodyte's meal for the night was a non perishable. It was simple, straightforward and sure. There was no opening for mistrust with a product of such caliber. For all the troglodyte knew, the curtained fridge era may be his last. A non perishable could see two or three more. So the troglodyte always ate like it was sacrament. Not concerned with the taste he was able to eat sacramentally. He would have his non perishable straight, with water and honey on the side. Honey was a favorite of the troglodyte's, though he couldn't explain why. But he knew that he must have it or not have it all, as is the case with any acquired tastes. So he chose to have it. At least until he had some other options.

There were no dishes and no dinner rush, so the troglodyte was able to count his steps. He tailored each step to accompany a breath. Hoping the rhythm would facilitate better digestion. It took forty steps to go from the kitchen to the bed in his room, where he lay down with unimportant thoughts. To keep thoughts of no consequence, he continued the count in bed even after footsteps were no longer heard.

The pre-sleep ritual was effective as long as the troglodyte didn't lose count while still awake. In those cases he would leave his bed and pace around the room. This sharpened his faculties as well as restarting the count in a familiar way. When he returns to sleep he should be able to

stay vigilant and remember the count until he forgets it
naturally again.

. . .

The troglodyte had walked to his mailbox three times the
next day. He strained his eyes focusing on the glare from the
signs and mailbox, with promises he'd test himself on days
to come. Degree of difficulty dependant on what time he
went to the mailbox, if the signs were turned and whether
they had shifted in the ground. He didn't start that first day
with a written record or tally.

Seeing spots still, it took the troglodyte a few minutes to
find the start to the path he was clearing. He didn't stop
making progress until he was able to see the town from the
cover of trees. He then walked the messy carpet back to his
house. When he was close enough he made a bundle of
sticks and carried it out of the wood.

Inside he took out a plastic carrying contraption. Which
was a singed, logo ridden, plastic fused shell of all the
leftovers from the water bottles and the cases they came in.
The soft plastic was used in layers and formed the exterior.
The harder plastic was shredded and burnt together on the
inside, making it flexible yet sturdy. He used his bag to
gather the downed branches, twigs and rocks. He walked up
and down the path, and up and down again, until he had
walked an equal distance both ways. Then discarded the
brush in front of his house. When finished he returned the
satchel to its resting place, which doubled as it's operating
table. The table is brown, has burn marks and smells terribly
of burnt plastic. The satchel held up so the table was not
over-tasked.

The troglodyte then confronted the mess outside. He had
kept adding to the pile, so that now when he looked at it he

couldn't see it as anything but that. He separated the stones from the sticks, then grouped according to size. Now it was no longer a mess but would be a project continued on another day. If he were to see the rearranged brush after having not thought of it, it would be a reminder that he had left it as it was so that he could make sense of it.

...

When the couple arrived at the house they noticed the sticks and stones, and marveled at the artistic mind of the troglodyte. They previously thought that they could only respect landscaping decisions that professionals who were paid well made. They hadn't thought much in the week leading up to the visit with the troglodyte, but the hearth of his home triggered something in them. They had had no trouble finding the place. The troglodyte had followed the directions he gave them when constructing the path. Nor were they troubled by the backward facing signs on the way.

The couple knocked on the troglodyte's door and felt the wood almost give in. Rain would fall off the roof and soak the door with winds blowing directly at the house. It wasn't raining on that night. There were some nights, but mostly days, when the troglodyte would brave a storm and practice entering and exiting a room. It was theatrical, different every time, and a cheap thrill. Emotions could accelerate from exhilarated to depressive, manically glad to incensed. Nature keeps one in the moment.

The troglodyte answered the door by waving the couple in. With his other arm he lifted the coat rack beside him, stepped back to let them enter the house fully, and put the coat rack down. Now when he closed the door they would both have plenty of room to stand. Arms by their sides. The troglodyte and the couple exchanged pleasantries before the troglodyte showed them out of the house to the patio in the backyard. They sat on cushions which the troglodyte had repurposed from his tanning bed and talked. The troglodyte asked most of the questions. The couple gave satisfactory answers. The questions were intended to produce the most amount of small talk possible. When you have all the time in the world to think on difficult subjects it is amazing what you'll miss. Any questions directed to the troglodyte were deflected and he made sure to steer them back to the most mundane of topics.

The couple enjoyed the small talk, wondering to themself if it was a more holy form of dialogue. Perhaps cushions were a divine way to sit as well. The couple had every right to have these thoughts, though the troglodyte never professed to have higher knowledge of any kind, but had been oddly unconcerned with his appearance. Some of the small talk centered around eating, and before any recipes could be brought up or any serious reviews given of restaurants, the troglodyte left briefly to prepare food for his guests. He returned with three bowls of soup, water and honey. The three ate together in silence. After the last spoonful was slurped, the troglodyte proposed a walk.

The couple agreed and were led back through the house, so dishes could be put in the sink, and out the front door. The troglodyte asked them to stay put while he went to get a light for the walk. He left the couple on his doorstep, went around the house and retrieved the light from dinner. Continuing around his property he turned all the signs so they faced away from his house. The couple appreciated the extra time they had to admire the brush out front.

When the troglodyte returned to the couple, he suggested they count each step taken and walk very slowly. The couple agreed, having some secondhand knowledge of walking over hot coals and unable to break from their delusion of the troglodyte. They were led down the path to civilization with conversation about various sounds of animals nearby and whistling winds. The couple could have found the way on their own, but the troglodyte wanted to make sure they got back to town and had not just said they were going. He said a confusing farewell to the them, turned around and began to walk back to his house. The couple dealt with this abrupt goodbye as parents deal with their child going off to college. Waving their hands for a very long time, saying they'd miss him and hoping he'd write. The troglodyte did not look back at the couple and after a little while they decided to go home.

The couple weren't known as the best gossipers in town but were not pariahs either. They went their separate ways to work the morning after, but relayed the same story to those who were friendly towards them. News spread of the small talk that was shared at the troglodyte's abode. Itself becoming the small talk of the town. Conversations were carried out verbatim by people as they passed one another.

Some would say something said at the beginning of the evening. Others started with the discourse on food. If two townsfolk passed each other and neither wanted to initiate the small talk, and if no third party was nearby to prod them in the right direction, one could still save face by talking at their back. Just as the couple had while the troglodyte was leading them to the patio, and also when he said his farewell. Lapses in time were not important in this re-creation ritual, so even if the troglodyte had not responded right away on that night, when he was portrayed he continues the conversation in a more agreeable manner. In the cases of the speaker talking at the about faced troglodyte, the actor responds either with the greeting or the question for a stroll. The parties continue with the script for as long as they think necessary. Back talkers, because of their lack of initiative, may cycle through many times. Whereas more confident folk start the conversation at a point of their choosing and break the conversation off once responses seem to more accurately represent that night. Pauses for thoughts.

The office workers were of the town folk but were placed above the town folk, both in their building and their own minds. They too participated in the small talk of the day and some were even non initiators when outside the office. Incapable of being stagnant and with a loose definition for innovation, the office workers developed their own shorthand for the customary greeting. It took from the gestures made by the troglodyte and his guests. One worker would pantomime opening a door, grabbing a coat rack, taking a step back and putting the coat rack back down. The other worker would pretend to cross a threshold and wave their arms to show they had plenty of room to stand. The shorthand followed the same structure as the verbal exchange. The gestures were made in a chronological fashion, with a steady wave followed by a door opening.

The higher up that had found fault with the troglodyte was having an emergency meeting on the third floor. He had heard that the troglodyte was back in town and could not be dissuaded from that notion until others had joined him in the room. When another worker told him that the troglodyte hadn't been seen for a few days, he started to cool off and think rationally. Checking his computer he found confirmation that the troglodyte's property had been zoned. Not able to understand how the meeting of the couple and the troglodyte was able to take place, it was decided that, just like last time, they would send someone out to do their bidding.

They picked an employee who had to wear a name tag because her illegible handwriting was slightly better than whatever accent she had tried and stuck with since her job interview. She made it out of town with no fewer than twenty opportunities to small talk and arrived at the signs surrounding the troglodyte's property. She had not been the one to put them there, but had been given all the details, and could not see any foul play. If the couple had seen these signs there was no way that they would enter the property. Even if the troglodyte were leaning upon one of the signs, inviting them inn, they still wouldn't have entered. Those who take signs lightly are seldom spared misfortune.

When she got back to the town she exchanged the small talk, more curt than before so she wouldn't get distracted, and soon was learning that no news is good news for the higher ups. They prided themselves for being in the know, so had she returned with a surprise they'd have been deflated. The woman was thanked and asked that the door be shut behind her when she left. They began talking of unimportant things which led to them pumping their egos with the successes of their new task force. When another situation arises they would pluck another random office worker to help them. And should things not go well on a mission, the employee could always be disaffiliated, if not fired completely, keeping the success rate high. It wasn't long before new ideas for the troglodyte started flowing between the higher ups, who were feeling they could do no wrong. Unfortunately they had been behind closed doors for too long and didn't realize all their employees had gone. They had an envelope signed and sealed but no one to deliver. They left it on the desk of the sign installer with a note that said to put it, the envelope, in a makeshift box atop one of the posts left at the troglodyte's property.

⑧

The sign installer woke to a splitting headache and didn't feel like removing the warning label on his pain relief, so he covered it with his thumb. He was a chef in the office building and something of a legend. No one saw him very often in the kitchen nor did they see him deliver his food. If customers had been familiar with his work he could have received compliments. His dishes never heard complaints in confidence after diners paid respect to the chef they thought had made it. Most of the office chefs in town have underlings that would dispense their creations but some chefs would make the rounds every once in a while.

So when the chef saw the note left on his desk, his jacket was thrown back on and he went to the last place his handiwork had been noticed. He counted the posts and knowing there should be one more than he had left, looked for that which was unlike the others. He found the mailbox and delivered the envelope, taking the note for himself. He wasn't sure how much mail the troglodyte was getting and couldn't be sure the troglodyte would check the box. He lifted his knee and kicked at the mailbox until there was a noticeable dent.

. . .

The mailbox caught the troglodyte's eye from a distance. The glare was different and caused him concern. He knew he had been observing light at around the same time each day, and though he didn't have a watch, muscle memory was preparing his eyes for pain.

When the troglodyte was closer to the mailbox and was able to see it with a fresh pair, his first thought was that a bird had flown into it. His next thought, since he saw no feathers or signs of an accident, was that something probably dragged or flew away with the bird. He absentmindedly began to reach for the mailbox's trap before pulling his hand away. Whatever had found the bird before him would most likely think it fertile hunting ground and may have claimed the mailbox as it's own. The troglodyte went from a blissful state of non thought to one of abject paranoia in an instant. It took him some time before he could resume admiring his creation.

There are many who keep their sanity by having an abundance of problems. Once a problem is solved there is a void left. This problem was one the troglodyte decided he would keep with him for a while. Not to check his mailbox for a few days.

He paid close attention to the mailbox for the next few days rather than just the glare cast off of it. Smelling the post and surrounding area for signs of life were added to his routine, and when he felt safe, received the letter.

He cut the envelope open with a pocket knife and let the contents fall in front of him onto the ground. A letter and a pin with the town's name and year it was established were enclosed. The letter began to fly away and probably would have went faster had it known the alternative. Unaware of its substance with no way to plead to the messenger not be shot. The troglodyte frantically reached for the paper, getting his first surprise in catching it easily and read what it said out loud.

'To whom it may concern, it has recently become a concern of ours that you have opened your borders. We did not receive adequate notice that this action would be taking place and would like to firmly state that we do not condone these activities. We ask that you appear before our town's council so this matter can be resolved. You will find a pin enclosed with the letter. If not, we ask you please do go find it. This pin will gain you access to our offices. You'll know the building. When you arrive make your way to the fourth floor and to the back of the line outside of the council's chambers. We look forward to being formally acquainted. -The concerned.'

The troglodyte frowned. First at himself. Then towards the letter. And finally in the direction of his mailbox. All the pride and joy previously derived from the sender-receiver was replaced with doubt. Would he have been able to spare himself from this meeting if he had never made the mailbox? He certainly wouldn't have received the letter. Or on the off chance he had, the delivery would have had to have been done in person, and barring that the deliverer didn't turn and run after handing him the subpoena, he would have been able to dispute. He could have argued with the messenger.

The letter didn't have a date for him to appear, so the troglodyte took the brush in front of his house and started a fire. The letter burned easily but the pin took more of an effort. The tin began to fold in around the needle and was easily spotted in the pile of ash once the smoke cleared. He took the refurbished pin and weak with exhaustion went to his fridge, grabbed a water bottle, held it to his neck and went to sleep.

In the middle of the night the bottle broke under the weight of his neck, soaking his head and shoulders. He toweled off, counting each stroke, and had no trouble getting back to sleep. He knew he had dried off completely and was surprised in the morning to find a puddle still around his head. Later in the day when the information wasn't as interesting to him, did he realize that he had broken into a sweat during the night. He didn't wonder what had caused his discomfort as he entered the office building.

⑨

No one paid him any mind as he walked through the office, or at least none said what they were thinking to him as he headed for the stairs. The fourth floor workers were no different, and it wasn't until he was standing in line that he was struck by conversation from an elderly woman. She told him how she was summoned to dispute an aggravated assault claim against her from an employee at a restaurant. She had had a good number of positive experiences at this restaurant, until one night she believed she suffered food poisoning from meat served under cooked. Her symptoms lasted a clean week and each time she had to run to the toilet she cursed the place that had made her sick, vowing revenge. On the first day when she felt marginally better she returned to the restaurant and managed to give one of the employees third degree burns. She ordered a coffee and when it arrived had thrown it in her servers face. Her logic was that since she got something under cooked, or not as hot as it needed to be, she would return the favor with something that was allowed to get too hot. She believed in both instances the restaurant was to blame, but admitted being grateful because it allowed for her return visit to go better than planned.

The troglodyte liked the woman but didn't care for her story. At no point in the retelling had she mentioned going to see a doctor or what the restaurants food safety rating was. Food safety warnings weren't in town thirty years ago but the troglodyte noticed them immediately upon reentry, and thought them to be very useful, pertinent information. The woman asked what the troglodyte's excuse was for wasting a day. He said he was just doing as he had been asked. The woman didn't like his answer and looked up and down the hall for anything to help make light of the affront. Seeing the woman's displeasure and not wanting to be made a victim, the troglodyte allowed the people who had starting queuing behind him to now cut in front. They soon were talking amicably with the woman.

When the troglodyte finally entered the council's chambers, after a full day of irritating talk with strangers and letting them pass him in line, he did not feel as sharp as he would have liked. The council introduced themselves, and he to them, before asking for a respite and possible rescheduling. The council agreed without needing to give it any thought, they had an open door policy and nothing was ever scheduled, and wished the troglodyte a speedy recovery.

As the troglodyte walked out of the room he saw a line of expectant people, with faces which anxiously asked if his news was bad. The troglodyte smiled as he walked and the people in line were reassured. Perhaps they would make it out of their situations, and at that moment the troglodyte was a beacon of hope. His win would be another's woe. Woe to them who didn't know. In the moments after, while the troglodyte was walking home or even had arrived, he was cursed by the people learning their situations would do anything but improve. They didn't don smiles when their matters were left unresolved.

...

At home, the troglodyte fixed himself a non perishable and waited for his tanning spot to become a place to star gaze. The troglodyte had enjoyed looking at the stars until he started to find comfort in it. Then he could never truly enjoy them again. The stars were a collective, though there were great distances between them.The troglodyte respected anything that was able to become a collective. He himself had been a founding member of an organization, whose sole purpose was to recycle and repurpose plastic on a small scale.

His satchel was one such prototype that had never fully taken off. If his plastic satchel had been a success he may have never sought seclusion, and a clean break from the busy world of sales and marketing. He had had to find a different reason to get away. The design wasn't necessarily flawed and the Plastics Repurposed Group, as they called their firm, had no problem selling what products they had. It was the amount of labor required that cut away from any profits.

There were four members of the PRG, troglodyte included. Even at that stage in his life, the troglodyte had not been greedy and had no problem absorbing the costs. The other founders lived different lifestyles and had taken on the venture hoping to better the environment, but still expected some tangible returns. They would take time off from work to work on reusing the plastic, and would return home tired and burnt out. One by one the founders eventually decided to give up on their idea of being essential to making essentials by the fusing of burnt plastic. The troglodyte was given all their unused plastic and prototypes so that they couldn't easily be asked about their failures.

The troglodyte repurposed all of the plastic, making some unique items and burying the rest in the ground. Since the troglodyte seldom had guests he had not tested his theory, but on some days, after a particularly long stint in his chair by the fridge, he swears he can see vapors coming up from the burial ground. It being night and still without guests, the thought of a collective of rising vapors was nowhere in his mind. The stars gradually faded from view as he fell asleep. He would wake to the black sheep.

Rubbing the dust from his eyes, the troglodyte saw his mailbox being thrashed about by the wind. The path in the direction of town had created a wind tunnel. It had been active all morning. The troglodyte had been shook awake and was grateful that more damage hadn't been done on his property. It wasn't long before the mailbox came apart all together and the troglodyte watched as the pieces went their separate ways. None of the splintered mailbox pieces found their way to the sorted sticks. That would be another project for the troglodyte.

The troglodyte had been growing too accustomed to his refined way of living, and the windstorm fiasco and subsequent disaster was just what he needed. As he kept getting hit in the face with dust, he decided to make himself and his property a more formidable adversary against nature. Taking some curtain off his fridge and grabbing two empty plastic cases, he headed to his workbench.

His workbench was just what he needed it to be. On it were a propane torch, used when a lighter wouldn't do, a knife used on most every project, and a measuring tape. Remnants of his last project were splayed upon the table. The troglodyte forced out of his mind the struggle he'd been having with designing a water bottle filter. Thinking he may have time after this project to start up on that one again concentrated his thoughts. Taking two water bottles he cut the bottoms off, doing his best to make the edges smooth and even. He then cut small pieces of cloth from the curtain and wrapped them around the open sides of the bottle bottoms after punching two holes into each of the bottles. Gutting the top of the water bottles, he then made the plastic as flat as it would allow and began cutting it into fine strands. With each water bottle he was able to produce twenty strands. He set eight strands aside, which he would later halve and quarter, to make the bridge for the glasses. He took each strand one by one and burned both ends with a lighter. He repeated this process until he had two decently sized bits of plastic. Putting the repurposed plastic through the holes of the bottles he assembled a pair of goggles. Not quite content with his creation, since the cloth had no way of staying on the lenses, he cut more cloth from the curtain and took the thread out. He then sewed the cloth onto the frames and set out to brave the weather of the day.

His next task would be to create a mailbox that either could face the elements, or not be subject to them. The mailbox either needed a shield or to be completely underground. No longer needing the workbench, he left everything as he found it after the goggles were finished, and got hit by the door on his way outside.

Had the troglodyte not fashioned himself goggles, there would have been no way for him to be out in the sandstorm. He was buffeted by pebbles as he made his way slowly across his property. The signs that the office worker had put up were very close to coming out of the ground. This time by no fault of the troglodyte. Noticing the craftsmanship of the signs, the troglodyte couldn't help but feel impressed with himself. He was braving the elements with vigor and resolve, while the signs were close to conceding. As he began closing in on where his mailbox had stood, he began to crouch. Adopting this new way of walking he found it easier and less dangerous than before. He made it to the post, realized his best bet would be to make the new mailbox under the ground, and walked to the nearest sign. Popping the sign out of the ground, he walked back using it to shield his face from debris. He put a corner into the dirt and started digging, throwing the excess over his shoulder. Since the wind was as strong as it was he didn't need to be that accurate with his throws, but hardly any fell back in the hole.

Only when there was a good amount of dirt surrounding him did he break and ponder the next step. The troglodyte liked a hole in the ground as much as the next person and thought it a shame to have it desecrated. So giving up the idea for a traditional mailbox, he wondered if it were possible to alert any postal workers that it was in that hole he wanted his mail delivered. He would use the sign to make slits along the wall of the hole but needed to dig himself more space to do so. When the hole had started to become a ditch, he jumped in. While inside the ditch he made stairs so that there was easy egress and crafted forty mail slots. Fearing that the slots may disappear after a heavy rain, the troglodyte pitched the outside of the ditch with the dirt that had been removed. In the mounds surrounding the ditch he wrote 'mail' and squatted the sign back to its place.

The sandstorm had subsided somewhat in the time it took for the troglodyte to make the adaptations to his property. He could now see two of the other signs, both on the ground, so neither was pointing to or away from his house. He planted the sign he was carrying so that it faced towards his house, and walked around his property doing the same with the others. When he got to the last sign he went into town.

1⓪

His trip to the office was much like the previous one,
and so he arrived to the line on auto pilot. When the chamber
doors opened he made eye contact with one of the council
members. Moments later he was rushed past his peers
awaiting counsel. The council asked for his name and once it
was given, they started to talk border policy. The troglodyte
believed that since it was his property he could do as he
pleased. The council believed that since it wasn't their
property, it was their right to be involved. The troglodyte
suggested day passes if he were expecting guests. The
council theorized mandatory supervision. The troglodyte
asked what they would do if they were in his place. The
council questioned how they could ever stoop so low.

It became obvious to the troglodyte that the council had
no intention of appeasing him, and would do whatever they
could to keep him in isolation. He thanked them for their
time but not what they did with it. He left the chambers
massaging his temples, which signaled to all those waiting
what they should expect. When he got to the stairs he went
down one flight and stepped on to the third floor lobby. The
set up was the same as the floor above. The troglodyte
appreciated the uniformity of the building. The building was
divided but was made stronger through each part.

The troglodyte walked to a line of people, who apart
would give less power to that which they were waiting on.
Since he had been called into the chambers without waiting
above, he decided to pay his respects and wait in the line
below. When got to the halfway point in line he was
approached by security. They asked him to leave. The
troglodyte tried his explanation, promising he had no intent
to take up any time of the waited-ons, and, that when he was

summoned he was going to turn around and leave. Not good enough for security, who said that even if he wasn't wasting anyone's time he was still wasting space. The troglodyte had no argument, thought of his house, and before long was in bed counting his breath.

...

The troglodyte remembered his dreams the next morning so took no time to make sense of them. He didn't usually recall his dreams and was usually able to carry on with his day without their insight. If something were to happen in the troglodyte's waking life that had already happened in his dreams, he would feel déjà vu just like everyone else. However, the troglodyte's response from there was not involuntary. Where others may get a shiver or goose pimples, the troglodyte broke into a sweat, and was unreachable as calculations spun around his head. The sweat was his body responding to fear. Since the fear was self-induced, the sweat was willed. To see two snowflakes that are identical is scary. To see two different identical snowflakes falling concurrently is terrifying.

The troglodyte spent most of the morning in his chair watching the sun climb. When dusk fell he clumsily got out of the chair and asked some invisible hand where the day had went. He decided he wouldn't be able to sleep that night, and headed to a place of eats. After walking the distance and developing an even greater appetite, he stopped at a deli where the food safety warning was passable. The troglodyte ordered only so much, so that even if the rating was false he wouldn't get sick from eating it. He paid more than enough. With one foot already out the door he asked if there were any places that had good dessert. The person running the register, who hadn't moved once while he was there and so appeared to be a torso sitting atop the counter, said no and didn't work his face's muscles any more.

The troglodyte went to the next store front that was open, this one a mart without meat, and bought a piece of chocolate. Consuming it only made him hungrier. He bought more pieces, this time in a pack. He picked and pecked at the pack of pieces poking out from his pocket as he walked. Once satiated, he scrambled for a destination for his stroll so that he wouldn't start to cramp. His thoughts turned to entertainment.

He hadn't paid to be entertained for more than thirty years. He wondered if they made entertainment for people like him. The troglodyte carried his excitement all the way to the theater and grinned as he grabbed the ticket. He wasn't familiar with any of the films, so went with the cashier's recommendation. She suggested a movie called 'Dog, Man's Vest Friend.' It was about a blind boy who would overcome his troubles, achieving fame and fortune, by taking to gambling and cards with help from his seeing eye dog. The troglodyte found the movie enjoyable, but was afraid to look at any of the people in the theater with him. He hadn't paid to be entertained for more than thirty years. He deserved to have a moment. The troglodyte took some of the theater with him when he exited, out of practice stepping over popcorn and candy wrappers.

The troglodyte went back to the deli to say he had found dessert. The employee took one look at him and believed the claim. The troglodyte waited for service. When it didn't come he fought silence with silence. He didn't mention he slandered their name earlier. Or that he cautioned the marters to refuse service to anyone who worked at the deli.

1

The troglodyte was beginning to find it easier to be involved in confrontations, gaining more experience with each trip in to town. He now had no problem disengaging conversation with the town folk when they began to small talk. He could leave them, and they would carry on both sides of the conversation by themself, at a pace faster than before, hoping to hit on a favorite part of the troglodyte's so he may jump in and make them feel comfortable. When he visited the office he was antagonistic and delighted in small victories when flecks of truth revealed. It was light, playful banter he spat, until it wasn't, and hardships were credited for making the person standing before him. If the troglodyte should feel insulted, having none other to blame but himself, and something personal is coughed up, it is to be dissected and studied.

The troglodyte was only half victorious on trips to the office though, still not finding a resolution to the problem he was told he had. The council reassured the troglodyte that his was a special case, and although it was taking a while to resolve, they were using their time wisely. Border policy is for humans but not of humans was a mantra they would use to combat the troglodyte's questions. They spoke of a time when there were no borders, and how the people living in those conditions teetered on insanity. They told a tragic story of a whale who resisted borders. They concluded each meeting by asking the troglodyte to think about all that was said, and that they would reciprocate. The troglodyte followed their orders, taxing as they were, and found no thought more unimportant than the last.

They weren't the worst thoughts he could have in his head while waiting in line, which had also become a game for the troglodyte. Familiar with all five floors of the office and the roof, the troglodyte would mull over his conversations while trying to not be spotted by any of the security on their respective floors. Worst come to worst he would be asked to leave, which he already planned on doing, and he could shake his thoughts from the property, so when resumed would be all the more cogent.

He never recognized anyone from the lines he occupied on the street. He wondered which people were having the harder day, the queued or the on the move. He couldn't be sure, but had a strong suspicion that the council talked in the same strange way to everyone they encountered, even if his was a special case. If the queued enjoyed that type of conversation, finding it insightful and intelligent, the on the move were missing out. If the movers were en route to be shaken by an even more stimulating discourse, then the queued would have chosen the wrong battle. The troglodyte was only able to have his inner monologue because he had already digested what the council had said.

The troglodyte made his way back to the property, greeting idle chatters curtly. He checked his mail ditch and was happy to see it had compacted. The dirt less trampled contrasted with the beaten down and gave the ditch character. He hadn't gotten any mail and checked the perimeter of the ditch to make sure his instruction was still there. He went into the house flustered.

He had no reason to expect mail, as it is with most people, but still expected there to be mail, as it is with most people. If he could not get mail, he would get there to be mail. He found a needle that could sew, and a water bottle, and began to work. He first had to get the label off the water bottle then find a way to hold the label taut. He tacked the label to the wall using two medium length needles that could sew, so that the label rested halfway to the house. The holes were diagonal from each other, with one in the top left corner and the other in the bottom right. This done so that when his message was done, depending on the size of the letters and brevity of the content, these placement holes could be used as punctuation. He took another sewing needle and carefully began to poke at his letter. It took as many repetitive movements to write 'don't forget about me' as it would have taken to pen a letter of a much greater length. He then positioned the placement holes accordingly, to make an upside down exclamation mark at the beginning, and one right side up at the end. He divided a bottle and put the halves under something of weight so that when flattened he could put the letter inside. Once inside and as close to air tight as possible, the troglodyte would burn both ends to preserve the message. Doing as much as he could at the moment for the letter meant having to practice patience in dealing with the post.

    ...

    The troglodyte found the most effective way to be patient was to sleep. Even if stress seeped into his dreams, and the troglodyte woke from a nightmare, he still would have passed time without forcefully exerting his will. The troglodyte woke at some point and thought more weight could be added on top of the bottle halves. He then kicked himself, thinking there was no guarantee they would maintain their flattened state better than if he allowed them the time to rest, so he forced himself to sleep. Only a child can get away with asking how long to be patient for. Everyone else accepts it.

The two halves of plastic were as flat as they were going to get under the troglodyte's watch, so he removed the weight from on top of them. He hoped with the letter laminated it wouldn't be considered trash. Before leaving to deliver his post he repeated the process of making an envelope, so that if the time came when he would need to send another, he would be prepared. The troglodyte left his property with envelope in front pocket, in case yesterday's chocolate still lingered as scent. When he came to the ditch he put the mail into a slot on the side farthest from his house, closest to the town. He took the post that had once held up his mailbox and walked it off his property. With no purpose for the post, and no destination for it's journey, he walked aimlessly until a sound interrupted his thoughtless escapade. A child was cycling towards him. Their approach was marked by ticking cards in their spokes. Once more distance had been closed, most of which was done by the cyclist, the troglodyte yelled a greeting. He was met with more rhythmic ticking. Only when the child was face to face with the troglodyte did they stop pedaling and acknowledge him.

The child told the troglodyte an actual walking stick would save his hands from misery. The troglodyte told the child if they wanted to make noise riding they should get a motorcycle or car. The child proposed a trade with the troglodyte, asking about the post he was carrying. The troglodyte asked the child what they had to trade. The child um hummed. The troglodyte arrived at an idea for the trade faster than the child but waited to bring it up. Thinking the child would benefit from the creative stress put on their brain. When the child had finally exhausted all their possibilities for a trade, and the troglodyte's legs had begun to cramp, the troglodyte told the child about his mail situation. A deal was devised. The child would periodically check with the mail sorters for any of the troglodyte's mail, deliver that to the ditch, and bring anything the troglodyte left behind to it's designated areas. The child continued riding after agreeing to the trade. The cards were barely audible as the post dragged from the back of the bicycle.

The troglodyte walked as if a huge weight had been lifted off of his shoulders, without direction. He passed the deli, the town's center, and the office buildings on the outskirts. He found himself in a residential area where houses were homes, or at least provided the chance to commute.

The wife of the couple, who was divvying up water between plants, said she felt the troglodyte's presence before she noticed him. Her head being towards the ground, she probably saw him in her periphery. When the troglodyte heard her call, which confirmed it was her and not some scrupulous doppelganger, he approached the white picket fence that was her trellis system. She reminisced of the time that they had all spent together, while he nodded appropriately. After enough time had passed to make the question valid, she asked of herself where her manners had been and invited the troglodyte in for refreshments. The troglodyte could not refuse, for she had just found her manners and that called for something.

The host lit a cigarette and drew closer an ash tray that said 'dust to dust' in bold letters. She offered him a smoke and the troglodyte came alive for the first time that conversation. He asked a question. She told him the body is a temple and smoke is used in many temples to ward off bad spirits. She blew smoke in his face but the troglodyte didn't flinch. He accepted the cigarette and lit it with his own lighter.

They looked at each other while they smoked, neither saying much. Both moving the lighters around their fingers. Sometimes placing it on the back of the hand to be flicked up end over end and caught again. Once they had given up the ghost, the trail of smoke having left the host, she caught him up on things he hadn't asked. Which was fine with the troglodyte. He was punching down and using a toothpick to joust at the morsels that had been taken out. Cheese, crackers and thin sliced meats never stood a chance, once the troglodyte realized his chewing looked to her like nodding. Her manners had been exemplary after she found her footing and this was not lost on the troglodyte. When she had exhausted her monologue that might have been saved for him, and the troglodyte had cleared the silver tray of all the food and three more cigarettes, the troglodyte said his goodbyes and promised to return again. She returned him a big smile. Her hands were on her hips and she shook her head from side to side. It was as if she thought the troglodyte was a good rascal.

The troglodyte stayed on his friend's street, and walked until he came to a housing development that was yet to be constructed. There was a map of the town just outside the fence, with smaller maps available to take. He traced his finger along one of the smaller maps, going in between the creases so he could open it fully. With the map stretched out he was able to follow the correct route to the train station with his eyes. There was time enough in the day for him to make it there and people watch.

...

He hoped to watch the people inside of a train but could settle for watching their past selves. The slightly more anxious passengers who aren't sure their train will arrive on time were more predictable, less entertaining, than the passengers already on board who could only think of what they'd do when they get off.

The closer he got to the station, the darker the sky seemed to get. The train station entered his field of vision just in time to spare the map from getting wet. He wasn't in the rain for long and passed under the arched doorway leading into the station. From there he approached the ticket desk. When asked where he would like to go, he said anywhere but where he was, adding he'd like the possibility to return. The teller said there were no problems yet and produced a two way ticket for him. He argued he would only offer enough money for a one way ticket, since he was going the same way back. The teller on that day was a model employee. The troglodyte still ended up only paying one way.

     The teller told him where the best spot to wait for his train was, but suggested he try one of their vendors, if he could multitask. The food court smell was intoxicant enough to mollify any hunger he may have had. He entered the belly of the beast and found a bench that overlooked where his train would arrive.

The bench he sat on seemed like it could sit three people comfortably. The troglodyte looked around to confirm his theory. What he saw were three people pushing each other as they joked. There was a person with their back to the troglodyte who the troglodyte noticed as he was scanning the room. Even though the troglodyte had been wildly moving his head around, to survey all possible sitting situations, the person behind him hadn't glanced up once from their paper. Wondering what could be so interesting on the page, the troglodyte pretended to sneeze, jerking his head back as he did. He then quickly began apologizing before the man could even say a bless you. After the man did address the sneeze, he said it was neither the time nor the place to have to sneeze. It was not allergy season and they were away from allergens. The troglodyte excused himself and balefully put his head down to glance at the man's paper, saying if something gets in his eye he often has to sneeze. With the interaction over, the man returned to reading his paper. Focused on not focusing his eyes to the patterns of an optical illusion.

The troglodyte got up from his bench to talk to a woman. This woman had said bless you to the troglodyte during his ruse. He said thank you, which may have been a sin. Since he could have said so without getting up, he sat back down. She said she'd seen countless people sneeze at train stations before and never had they gotten any grief. She believed those same people could be around allergens in peak season and never sneeze. The troglodyte thanked her for speaking on his behalf and stood up.

...

The train arrived on time. The troglodyte was first to one of it's doors. People down the platform were also getting on, but the waiting area he left was empty. He took his seat, looked out the window, and the seat took him. He woke to the train coming to a grinding halt. Increased brightness followed.

A conductor walked past and got off the train carrying a backpack. She was cagey when asking for each ticket. She proved she was worth her salt when one teenager tried snubbing the ticket industry. The conductor didn't allow him passage and put the counterfeit in her backpack, to keep as a souvenir. The backpack was worn on her front, and having now been unzipped, provided the possibility of a mysterious threat. The teen didn't test the conductor, which tested the conductor's patience, and took back a written citation to their condemned seat. The offender would have to pay the amount of a two way ticket plus ten percent. They were required for community service for the length of the train ride times three. This was written on the citation.

When the troglodyte didn't stir from his seat, the conductor went to him and told him to wake up. The troglodyte took his head from off the window and blinked at the conductor to show no eyelid lag. He said he was going back the way he came and lazily pushed his ticket over. The conductor decided the troglodyte could stay on the train, so long as he kept his seat while any new passengers boarded. The conductor disappeared into the train. Shortly after the doors locked the troglodyte saw her walking off the platform in civilian clothes. The lights went out at about that time. The troglodyte was left to wait for the freshly shaven to start their shifts.

Unable to sleep after his nap, he did more waiting and looked out the window at the lit platform. There were no people to speak of. Viewing a clock took up his time, and he watched the minute hand until he could almost hear it tick. The clock let him know he overstayed his welcome, when the ticking continued but his eyes had not.

The teen was woke first by the conductor, who was the same as the night before, to a rap on the head and a pun on eggs. Then the conductor had the train woken by radioing the engineer. The troglodyte woke violently and really wanted to

remember what the last thing he thought about was before he
fell asleep. No one should have to wake like that.

The doors to the train opened, allowing passengers
waiting on the now somewhat crowded platform to board.
The troglodyte succeeded with his expectation of not seeing
any familiar faces at the first stop, or any one thereafter.
When he was back at the station he had departed from, he
and other passengers watched the transit authority board the
train. Words were had. First with their fact checker, then
with the skipper. The authority reread the offence and
punishment, to the delinquent, and asked if there were any
questions. The teen wanted to know why he wasn't asked for
questions from the start. The transit authority thought the
question was too needy and didn't oblige the beg with an
answer, instead writing in a notepad and visibly underlining
the sentiment repeatedly. The teen was escorted by the arm
off of the train. Passengers out of earshot when the charges
were read weren't sure whether to clap or protest.

When the troglodyte was back on solid ground, he went
to the teller booth that had caved to his stubbornness. It was
a different teller than the day before. The troglodyte felt he
could handle a loss. After trying to run the same reasoning
on the new teller that he had the old, he tipped the maiden
voyager for taking up their time, and left without buying a
ticket. The tip was declined at first, and was only accepted
after light argument.

. . .

The day was young. The morning growing older. So
when the troglodyte tried to get back to the office he found
they were closed for lunch. He couldn't make sense of how a
whole office, with presumably at least one chef on each floor,
could be out to lunch. He made eye contact with someone

walking nearby and asked if they could believe it. The troglodyte learned lunch taking was important in some cultures, the present one included. The troglodyte rephrased his question and asked how the office could be closed to the public because of lunch. The passerby began to get suspicious, and threatened to let the authorities know the troglodyte was trying to get a free meal. Anyone who knew how to plan a day around lunch would have belonged in the office, and the troglodyte's not knowing showed he was up to no good. The troglodyte began stammering, solidifying the passerby's disbelief. Who thought lying would come easily to all but the guilty, and that people were usually their most eloquent when talking of the table. When no words came to the troglodyte that couldn't be used against him, he stepped away from the office.

When the troglodyte had circled a closed down buffet a few times, he courageously asked another local when the restaurateurs would be back from lunch. She told him they were facing a lawsuit, and couldn't afford to pay legal fees and keep lights on at the same time. The restaurateurs were being taken to court for their claims to have an all you can eat buffet.

A child had been eating, while it's parents dined, and had swallowed a crayon while their mother was preparing them a plate. The child was taken to the hospital, very sick for some time. The parents were suing on that child's behalf. The family that litigates together, stays together. Their claim was that 'all you can eat' implies anything can be ate, and can be done so until one's had their fill. The restaurant's case could have been stronger, if not for their willingness to agree one was able to eat to their heart's content.

...

As the troglodyte sat at home enjoying one of his non perishables, in the office building, where regular work had now resumed, two constables were asking the council for the date they had last seen him. Not good with faces or names, the council was unable to provide any help. They were most useful if defendants prepared a file about themself. Since there was an open door policy, they seldom had the file ready. They told the constables that their most recent run in with the troglodyte could not have been more than two weeks ago, but definitely did not seem to be in the past week. The constables thanked the council members for all that they do, and told them to never stop improving.

Back at the station the constable partners rolled out the troglodyte's letter. They began to worry. If it was a ransom note it wasn't a very good one, which meant the ransomer was probably unstable and could be dangerous. There were no demands or a place for them to meet. They had questioned the young girl. She could only tell them that a man had given her the job of delivering and checking for mail in a ditch, by a house in the middle of nowhere. The constables knew the house. They wondered if the troglodyte's captor was having the girl check on the house to ensure no suspicious activity was carried out by law enforcement. They moved on when they realized the girl hadn't been told to contact the man after she delivered the note. The constables told their superior they had no new information about the case and headed out to the troglodyte's property.

They found the troglodyte's house as easily as his other visitors, and were surprised to see what they assumed was either the troglodyte or his captor. They approached the troglodyte with their guns drawn. They told him to stop, put his hands on his head, and make no sudden movements thereafter. The troglodyte had just about finished putting the last sign back facing away from his house, when the constables interrupted him. He let the sign fall and was compelled to comply with the constables. When they approached him and asked what business he had being there, he told them it was where he lived. He added, he made it his business to really live but had settled for just living.

The constables realized it was the troglodyte they were addressing, so holstered their guns and began deposing him. When it was clear parts of the situation had been misunderstood, the constables began to dread going back to the station. They had made a big fuss over nothing, which was worse for them than making too little fuss over something big. They told the troglodyte they would put in a good word in for him at the post office, but warned they were a strict, vengeful, exacting bunch. Said he'd do best not to cross them. As the constables left the troglodyte put the sign back in the ground, not flipping it as he intended.

The troglodyte went to the post office, searching for his for hire mail courier on the way. It didn't take long for the troglodyte to find her. He followed his ears. When he approached the child, she started to yell at him to stay away, amidst reassurances that she wasn't a snitch. She said she wasn't an informer and that it takes an incrimanator to know one. The troglodyte did his best to get a word in over her hysterical ranting. He had to continually start again with his explanation of the matter resolving. Whether this got through to her or she just got tired, she ended her conversation by saying that no longer would she deliver his mail. The troglodyte said fine, and didn't even ask for the sign post back, for failure to complete her contract.

At the post office the troglodyte was almost hit by a mail truck in the parking lot. The postal workers had trucks. The post office visitors were so familiar with the pairs that there was constant friendly horn honking. The troglodyte was distracted by the horns and was looking around for each source, until one was very easily identifiable. The honk continued past the troglodyte, and only stopped when the mail truck came to the end of the lot. The worker didn't want to appear rude to the innocents.

Once he was safe and the truck had rejoined traffic, the troglodyte went into the post office with his head bowed. He didn't look up until he was in front of a clerk. The clerk smiled at him as she said next, as was required, and then resumed her normal manner. She scowled when she heard the troglodyte's request to bring mail to a property outside of town. She scoffed when asked that it be left in a ditch. The troglodyte tried to save face, saying his original mailbox couldn't brave the elements. He lost said face when he had to cough up his box wasn't standard issue of the post office.

The postal workers could deliver mail to residents who didn't have one of their boxes, but gave them less priority. Their letters and fliers would go out for delivery and return at day's end, piling up until there was enough to justify giving premium benefits to inferior customers. The troglodyte persuaded the clerk to game the system, and give him inferior benefits for a premium. What he was asking was blasphemy to the post office,who, bless their hearts, believed there was no such thing as junk mail. The integrity of the mail won out over the clerk's pride. It was decided a worker would go to the property once a week. On weeks where the troglodyte came in to the office, the worker would not come.

The clerk gave him a piece of paper and stamped envelope, urging that he write a letter to himself to try out their services. She then excused herself from behind the desk to give him some privacy. She came back as soon as he had finished writing, asking if he had any help during the process, or if he were out of sight of the letter for any amount of time. The troglodyte truthfully answered in the negative. Someone behind him backed him up, which gave the clerk pause. She did take the envelope, put it in a tube and hammered her fist on to a button. Just like the gavel that also sends away. She then put a finger on a smaller button to start a recorder, and summarized everything that had taken place, and been discussed, since the troglodyte had begun to be served. When asked what the best way to reach him was, the troglodyte said by mail, which won him a genuine smile from the clerk as she stopped the recording.

1②

The troglodyte went back to his estate and cleaned the inside of his house. He first started by taking everything outside, disassembling some pieces of furniture so they'd fit through the doors. What was in the front of the house was moved to the backyard, so what was in the back could easily be brought to the front. He was careful to make sure anything with airborne capabilities was weighed down. He swept all through his house, sweeping through the house, figuring the wind would take care of any mess that might be swept on to the furniture.

He cleaned the glass on his house, both inside and out, using freshly squeezed juice from a lemon that wasn't. Other menial tasks were done when they came to mind. He considered them finished when he started bringing the furniture back into the house. Except for anything essential that had been taken apart, the troglodyte put back what he had taken out last, first. Since he had worked hard before so as to not need to now. His bed and workbench were left outside, while he stacked anything else in the front and the back walkways. Bigger objects on the outside were angled toward each door. The structure was hollow throughout.

He thought a cat could have a time of his creation, so he collapsed the better of the two, hoping he could recreate it in the wood by his house. He didn't mind sharing some of his possessions with nature, even though he knew it wasn't the best playmate. He reassembled his bed and workbench in the house, reacquainting them with the old furnishings. He made use of neither at the moment. Putting off the two things that perhaps needed him most. Sleep and repurposed recycled plastic. He took a water from the fridge, which was shaded because of the obstruction near the window, and had flashbacks of burn injuries. He went to the back yard barefoot to try to rustle up some sympathizers.

The sign facing in the wrong direction caught the troglodyte's eye. He appreciated the contrast. He went around the rest of the property and arranged for every other sign to be facing in an opposite direction. Which side of the sign he passed determined whether he was following it's direction, and he could only hope that on future journeys he would pick the right side. He promised himself that if the stress got to be too much with not knowing, the half of the signs that could be reverted back would be. This was still to be done for any visitors.

He had no answer for what to do about the signs near the ditch. He hoped the postal worker would be more decisive, or rebellious, than himself and could make a decision. He didn't think they would ignore the signs.

The troglodyte went back to his house and used the workbench to create a tube of plastic, large enough that an envelope could pass through cleanly. He made two elbows for the tube, and created two plastic bellows to help facilitate mail to the other side. He fashioned his equipment into the ground, after continuing the ditch in a trench to extend a little outside of the property. One bellows would be kept in his house. The other housed inside the tube for the worker. The postal worker would be sure to notice it when their mail was rejected. If they were curious enough to take out the bellows, they may be curious enough to give it a try.

The troglodyte left no instructions. It would take many trial and error runs for both of them to determine just how fast to pump the bellows. Too fast and the mail would fly right out the tube, or come back down the slope that is the elbows. Too slow and it wouldn't make it far enough to the other side.

1③

The next time the troglodyte went to the office, it was with the intent to invite the council over. So a discussion could be had as friends. The council agreed it could be done. Each member went through their calenders to find a date that would work. The troglodyte said, fine, to each date suggested as quickly as they changed their minds. When all their caveats had been added, he told them if they were looking for something to bring that wine would be good. He'd have had an easier time had he set the date himself. The secretary was invited as the troglodyte left the office. He had to start making preparations.

The first stop on his list took him to a MomAndPop furniture store. They didn't have the collapsible chairs he was looking for, so he left a box unchecked, and followed a river nearby until he came to a bait and tackle garage. He asked the purveyor where to find a chair like the one the homeowner was sitting in. He was told to look no further. The troglodyte explained that he wanted to buy a few chairs. Also some tent posts, so he could make a cloth taut enough to be used as a table. The seller said they had gotten the chair from a company his family and friends had given far too much money to. He would prefer the troglodyte to buy from him, even if it took lowering the cost. He didn't have the inventory on hand, but told the troglodyte to come back the next day. The purveyor would need some time to regurgitate the equipment from his friends.

The troglodyte thanked the man, started to walk away, stopped, and asked what experience the seller had with water purifiers. The seller said they had had a relative who was a founder of one of the big water bottle companies. They had known the secret of river to liver. It hadn't been passed down to his side of the family though, so now all they could do was drink the stuff and grieve.

The troglodyte's next stop was the church. Which he had no trouble walking into even though he hadn't been anointed in the faith. He knew other people were brought into the faith, some even for a second time, should they have fallen before and felt phantom limbs help them up. They would make up the difference for the troglodyte, one hand washing the other.

In the past when asked why he wouldn't be brought into the church, he gave different reasons, none less true than the last. There was a service going on as the troglodyte entered. He chose to follow customary ritual, so that he wouldn't offend anyone he could see. The church had always stressed he may not be a part of the church, but at least the church could be a part of him. There was a service already going on. The troglodyte took shelter close to where he had entered. The troglodyte studied the faces taking part in the service, and marveled at how reflexive their looks were with each other. The people were totally moved by one another and expression leaped from face to face. The troglodyte knew that he would have to be the one to break up their trance, and decided to do so on his own terms. Not by someone seeing him and mirroring his expression to the rest of the group.

He walked up to the crowd with shoulders back and chin up. He still looked to be skulking. He wasn't noticed until he tapped someone on the shoulder and asked who was in charge. The wrong person must have been in church. They pointed to the leader of the services. The woman saw the finger cast in her direction and told the troglodyte to join them, asking if he was in the faith. The troglodyte said no, but that the church was a part of him. The woman must have had different mentors, because she thought that thought profound. The troglodyte declined joining them, and asked if she counted chickens before they hatched. The congregation gasped in unison, but were settled down, and prompted to have some refreshments before leaving the church. The members now not so easily persuaded, taking the time to stand between the troglodyte and the woman to shake her hand. It was a strange power play, where each member looked at the troglodyte during the handshake, to show it was the top of their hand that would have been photographed.

When the crowd had left, the woman took the troglodyte to her office, which doubled as a surveillance room, and asked what was on his mind. The troglodyte got to his point after he was told that all the audio/video recordings were sent to be analyzed, at what is the theoretical capital of the religion. He wanted to know how the church's functions were catered, which got him the answer of, follow me. He was glad when the woman got up and left the office, reassured that the sustenance he was looking for would be tangible. She led him back to where he had interrupted the service, and explained that the church's members were the food providers and he was welcome to ask around for a hand out. His request was answered by two empathic women in their twenties, who saw the troglodyte's plight as their own. He gave them the time and place for his gathering, prematurely thanked them for their help, and left the church without any ritual. His departure would definitely be noticed. More than one person would probably atone for him.

1④

When the troglodyte went back to the bait and tackle shop, he was able to purchase eight camping chairs and eight posts for his table. The equipment looked to be brand new. It was explained to the troglodyte that most of the lot was purchased through reward points. The seller gave the troglodyte a written receipt, and wished him a good day. The troglodyte took what he could carry and went back to his house, feeling weird about having to go back to get the rest. He fought his fear and returned to get his stuff, half acknowledging the corny welcome back jokes he was assaulted with.

Before setting up any of the chairs or the table, the troglodyte took the receipt and practiced sending it through the mail chute. When he thought he had the hang of it, he shot the receipt out of the chute and collected it. He went into his house and struggled with how to set up the table. The posts couldn't go directly into the floor without tools, and he didn't want to rip up the floor to look for a more receptive surface. He went outside to begin moving the excess dirt from around the ditch closer to his house. When he had enough to secure the posts, he made the decision he would set his table up outside, and moved the dirt to the backyard.

The mound was ten inches deep and packed down another four once the posts were put in. He spread the canopy canvas around the posts, and weighted the corners so he assemble the table alone. He made sure the posts were high enough for the camping chairs to push in, before splintering an extra post to use for stakes. He covered the table with a curtain. In case of rain before, or during, the parade to his property.

. . .

The food arrived to the troglodyte's place first. Followed by the secretary. Then the three council members. Who walked side by side, staggered, so that they looked to be descending in height. The table held, as plates of shepherds pie and deviled eggs were placed on it. The secretary had her notebook out and was sketching the spread. Once all formalities had been acknowledged and a glass of wine was in the hand of all present, the two women who had catered excused themselves. Their work was never done. They wished the troglodyte well with his business. When the women were out of earshot, the council summarized their interactions with the troglodyte and detailed their plan.

First, the private property signs would be changed into ones with speed limits, or some type of animal crossing. Second, a road would be built, continuing in the vain of the path the troglodyte had made. Also, in the opposite direction. Connecting to a previously dead end road near a farm house. Third, the town would fund the project. The troglodyte needn't do almost anything. The road crew would be at his property within the week. The troglodyte was asked to have the new signs ready when they got there. The troglodyte's look of confusion was met with one of anticipation, by a council member who produced a putty knife.

The secretary, who spoke out loud what she was writing, though a few syllables behind, had been recording everything said. She made an audible note of the knife, stealing away from the moment the council member was eager to have. The council members said their piece, ate a fair share, and thanked the troglodyte for his hospitality. Reminding him that their doors were always open. The troglodyte showed them out, said he hoped it was the beginning of a mutually beneficial relationship, and went back to his company. He didn't interrupt the secretary as she typed up her shorthand. When she had finished, the troglodyte implored her to take any leftovers, wine included. She declined at first, asking the troglodyte to enjoy it with her, before feeling compelled to oblige . She left with a sour taste in her mouth.

...

The next morning the troglodyte was on the delivery route, he was working at scraping paint off of the signs. The postal worker stopped at the ditch. They stood over the apparatus and looked long enough at it for the troglodyte to begin to feel self conscious. He was making a lot of noise. The troglodyte watched the postal worker with bated breath as the bellows was picked up. The envelope was dropped in the chute. The bellows was pushed down lightly. The envelope got stuck in the middle. The worker circled the mail chute and looked from every angle to try and discover what happened. When the troglodyte started to dizzy, he yelled to the postal worker that he'd take care of it himself. The postal worker didn't ask how to work the mail chute. The troglodyte didn't offer any advice. With pity they looked at each other. Two old dogs with new tricks.

When the mail truck left, the troglodyte went to get his mail, without much difficulty, and put the unopened envelope into his breast pocket. He felt he knew what it said, and assumed the clerk held herself to the same standards she required of the customers.

It took the troglodyte three days to get the paint off of all of the signs. The work hadn't been hard. It had been time consuming, which stressed the troglodyte, who wanted to have the signs ready for the road crew whenever they got there. With a difficult job, experts may be brought in to hurry along the process, but any extra worker delegated is an added expense and must be taken away from more thought provoking tasks. The troglodyte did finish though, and so didn't worry about which way the signs were facing as he left to go into town.

He followed the route that had taken him to the bait and tackle garage, and continued following the river. Using smoke in the distance as a guide, within a couple hours he was at the water bottling plant. He approached one gate, found it to be the wrong one and passed all those that weren't the visitors entrance. He was greeted with a hand stamp and told the next tour would be start in fifteen minutes. The troglodyte sat with the other purists, until an enthusiastic middle aged woman introduced herself to those waiting, and their tour group was born.

The troglodyte stayed in the middle of the walking mass and had questions for the guide whenever he was prompted to give them. The tour guide provided obscure answers meant to satisfy and silence, finally offering that at the end of the tour questionnaires could be filled out. They would be addressed at the company's earliest convenience. The troglodyte broke off from the group, asking his peers if they'd just heard what he had, and continued the tour on his own. Taking in neither sights nor sounds. When the troglodyte got to the end of the tour's trajectory he filled out three pages, front and back, with questions about trade secrets. He gave his address, with a memo on the envelope which said 'if at first you don't succeed, try try again.' Parentheses were respectively added under 'you,' and, 'succeed,' with (I) and (receive).

The troglodyte left the processing plant. He took a hack to the town where his farmer neighbor to be lived. When he got to the town, which was eerily similar to the one he had been frequenting, either by design or the troglodyte's rose colored glasses, he asked around for the best way to get to the farmer's house. Also pointing him in the direction home. He followed the directions he was given and ascertained the correct route through consistencies in the answers he received. Using the bad suggestions with the good, the troglodyte would have been able to give the correct directions if asked, and found himself out in the pasture.

There were cows, chicken, sheep, and a donkey to greet him. The troglodyte had no experience on a farm, but the domesticated animals seemed to be docile and gave him no trouble. They were so nonchalant, that the thought of lining them up and using one bell to activate the others, think dominoes, passed through the troglodyte's mind. He would make sure to ask the farmer, or farm hands, if they had done this in the least offensive way possible. When he was at the doorstep of the farm house, he used the knocker and the door was answered shortly thereafter.

A boy opened the door, glanced at the troglodyte's fingernails, and said he wasn't interested in whatever it was he was selling. When the troglodyte explained he wasn't selling anything, and that he was there to talk about a new atlas, the boy was disappointed he didn't know the word. More disappointed that he couldn't shut the door and be rid of the troglodyte. The boy said he and his family weren't interested in any theological discussions and tried again to shut out the troglodyte. The boy's sister came down the stairs, spotted the troglodyte and yelled for her ma, bypassing any security the boy had thus provided. The girl went back up the flight, hoping her mother could handle the man unlike her brother.

The troglodyte wasted no time telling the mother of the recent development to his property. He was asked to slow down when the mother couldn't figure out exactly where he lived. She knew of the town that had commissioned the project, and knew where her house was, but couldn't picture a road connecting the two. The troglodyte could do nothing to tamper her confusion. The son came to her aide and spoke of possible routes through the woods he was vaguely familiar with. When her grasp of the situation had tightened, the woman turned on the troglodyte. She asked what exactly he wanted from her family. She warned they didn't take kindly to swindlers. The troglodyte said he wanted to be left alone once the road was built, and that any livestock that wandered onto his property were not his responsibility. The mother agreed, the cows didn't get to choose their own tattoos, and closed the door.

When the troglodyte was back in the field he was called after by a farm hand. The troglodyte stopped, and waited for the man to catch up so he could be caught up. The hand man said he didn't see many new faces around and that he hoped the troglodyte's presence was a good omen. The troglodyte told how he and the farm family were surrogate parents to a new road. Of an umbilical cord big enough to connect the two towns. The farm hand excited at the news. Just as countless others before him had, when they first hoped meaning could be found in freshly put down pavement. The hand man returned to the barn he had come from, with a little more pep to his step.

The troglodyte walked to where forest met field, and broke out of the pasture by making a single file path back to his property. The other town could make it wider and pave, as was to be done with the troglodyte's first path, or choose

to make their own route. When he was clear of the new path
and faced the rear of his house, he saw how out of place
were the table and chairs from a few nights ago. He packed
up all of the equipment. He dumped it in a corner of his
house.

The stowaway capability was impressive and paired well
with the troglodyte's open floor plan. Anything that could
take up considerable space was against a wall, with anything
that could be stacked, on top of that. The troglodyte decided
to make use of the clear space his eyes identified and started
to exercise. He did laps around the room. He did jumping
jacks and he did push-ups. The room became too hot and he
had to stop. He was pretty good about exercise. He had no
problem doing it. He didn't do it enough to remember when
he did it, what he did, and how he felt after, so his workouts
were sporadic. The troglodyte went outside for some light
stretching and hydrated his tired muscles.

Later, he showered. Then put on a t-shirt with a breast
pocket and a pair of carpenter pants, the style he now found
himself wearing every day, and sat down to read. The book
he was reading had been familiar to him, until his notes
covered whole pages entirely. He had crossed out the
original prose to make space for his own. What
understanding he had had of the book was long gone. The
scribbled insights provided no clues as to how to get it back.

He began to plagiarize the original words as best he
could and transcribed them into a notebook. He finished after
a few hours. Reading it back, he realized that if there had
been any substance left in the book, it would have taken
much longer to copy. He decided that copying his own notes
would be wise, so long as he were able to stay organized,

and began categorizing notes by color. There were black and blue and red notes.

He started with the red notes. Making sure not to add any new thoughts to what he was copying. The subject matter he was combing through was not necessarily high brow, but was made so by the lack of organization. Thoughts were scrambled. He remembered how steady his hand had been when he had taken them down. Moments of doubt are fluent throughout one's life but share the spotlight with assurances. The troglodyte at the time was just as confident as he was then, but now was able to confidently discern he had been practicing folly. When he goes back to this new notebook of his past musings, he will undoubtedly think there had to have been a better way. This deceit allows the self to strive for betterment. This deceit allows one to self correct as they see fit. His concentration was not broken from the transcription, but his interest waned with time, and he went out for some fresh air.

He walked around his property fondly remembering the signs, the discarded paint around the posts looking like tears. Personifying the posts led him to clean his gutters, revitalizing their tear ducts. He gathered the newly homeless wet leaves and brought them to the ditch. He dumped the leaves, and by the handful stuffed them into the mail slots. He realized that the slots would now be forever unoccupied because of the mail chute. He felt good about giving them purpose. He took the letter he sent himself from out of his pocket, opened it, and put sand and leaves inside, before sealing it. He put the envelope, along with a handful of leaves, into one of the slots so it was no longer visible. He hoped that it wouldn't ever be visible, and that the sand and leaves would help in it's degradation. He left the remaining leaves in the ditch, once all the slots were filled, and kicked them up by accident. He grabbed at one of the slots for balance. He found a firm hold. Once he regained the nerve to walk, he moved down the line, and tried his feet in the openings. Soon he was off the ground. He practiced climbing around for a little while, then went to his house to grab the goggles.

The troglodyte wanted to try the new talent with more difficult terrain, so wandered around in the woods until he found a suitable rock face. The goggles offered little protection. Subconsciously they helped the troglodyte tremendously. His thinking, whenever confronted with nature or forces outside of his control, was that if he showed mastery of himself, it would affect positive change. At the very least keep circumstances stagnant. His plastic goggles were an innovative take on both safety and function. The plastic protected his eyes from anything coming at him straight on. Also from above or below, because of how far they extended off of his face. Such a harmonious marriage usually can only be found in nature, and the troglodyte felt a kinship when he made use of his inventions.

He wasn't tethered while climbing the rock so didn't stray very far from the ground. Daring to think that crossing a small stream underfoot was an accomplishment, the troglodyte was able to justify leaving the comfort of home. If he were to fall, there was no current to take him. Nothing past his knee would get wet unless he was doubly clumsy. When he was successful, he tried no more risky maneuvering and felt complacent. No minor injuries to champion for his thoughts.

On the way back to his property he ran across a few hikers. They followed a trail of orange dots on the trees.

Somehow that made the troglodyte respect them less. The troglodyte hadn't noticed the marks on his way to the rock face. When they were pointed out to him he saw them clearly, even with the goggles on. The hikers told him the name of the trail, how long it was and where it went, and offered him food and drink. The troglodyte opened his palm receptively. Closed it when he discovered cuts, and blebs that might have been blisters, and said thanks anyway.The troglodyte told them where the stream was and that they could probably jump to the other side if they needed to cross it.

The troglodyte took the lone road. His parted company the hiked. He walked with his palms firmly pressed together, applying pressure to his wounds. Amplifying the pain so that he was back at his house in no time. He went to the back of his house to scavenge for cloth, so that he may wrap his hands. A second rush of adrenaline collided with the troglodyte as he sat with bandaged hands. He thought of the new type of movement he had found. He wondered what cavemen had thought about when they realized they could use their hands for eating. No longer needing to move their head as much. Gone were the days of snapping their mouth at everything that moved. No longer trying to catch birds out of the sky. Gone were the days of chasing animals down on the ground. With their prey caught, they ripped apart the flesh with their teeth. Their hands were used as anchors, for meat that didn't immediately come off the bone when shook by clenched jaw.

...

When the troglodyte's hands had healed a bit, he went along the first path, into that town, and stumbled all the way to church. The troglodyte interrupted another service. He ushered the two women that had catered his service over to him, and thanked them properly. He told them what floor the secretary worked on. They were free to go and ask about their dinnerware. As the troglodyte tried to leave, the woman with an office of her own stopped him and asked of his well being.

The troglodyte told her how his being had been. He asked if she had ever tried rock climbing. She said she had. She whispered it was called something different where she came from, and that it generally wasn't spoken about outside of very niche circles. She said she still had trouble discussing it openly. It had been a trying time in her life and was one of the primary reasons she joined the church. The troglodyte decided not to press her any further and was met with no resistance as he left.

After leaving the church, the troglodyte went to another frequented establishment. One where the audio/video recordings would be of little interest to anyone. He hoped to find an audience that could relate to his new fleeting passion. A portly fellow behind the bar said he also used to rock climb. He had given up the hobby when he discovered human ladders. He and his friends would go around to places that they couldn't reach, stand on each other's shoulders and be propelled to new heights. It sounded interesting to the troglodyte, so the man offered to show him how it was done. He called down the bar to a nondescript group, who answered and appeared to have been awaiting the question. In the bar was no place to showcase their talents.

The barkeep and troglodyte followed the group outside, where the performers prepared for an ascent. The barkeep was the heaviest and stood on the bottom, while the remaining members started to climb on top, and on top of each other. When the lightest was standing on a balcony on a third floor, the troglodyte could say he was impressed. When all the performers were back on the ground, the troglodyte asked if he could have a try. The barkeep turned into an enabler, and helped the troglodyte up to his shoulders, where the troglodyte was able to stand. Shakily at first, until he calmed his nerves.

The troglodyte had a lapse in judgement and tried to spur the barkeep on the shoulder. The shoulder couldn't be leaned on from that position, so the barkeep exclaimed in pain and the troglodyte was thrown. When the troglodyte was asked why he had spoiled the moment, one of the performers of the nondescript troupe came to his aid, saying everyone was already spoiled because most of those moments were not. The troglodyte didn't go back into the establishment, and went to an open space where he could sit and think.

1⑤

Plenty of people passed the bench the troglodyte occupied as he sat in the park. It was quitting time for many of the townsfolk. Storefronts were being closed for the day or opened for the night. The people paid no attention to the troglodyte. Their lives were busy. Perhaps they would have talked to him if they believed their schedules were fixed. Those are trying hours that pass just before and after work.

The troglodyte had stories about each of them. Not so detailed that they ever arrived at a destination. He pictured them as he saw them presently, on the move and chasing the clock. He had none of the people going to the same place, regardless of whether they were together when they passed him. Them were drawn apart by some emergency. He was broken out of his reverie by school children selling chocolate.

He asked how much they wanted for their product, having just missed the sales pitch, and then said it was much too much. The school children weren't used to being said no to, unless they raised their hands too often, and repeated the pitch for the troglodyte's now fresh ears. When they finished he said much too much again, and tried to haggle them down. He had no intention of buying any of the goods. He thought they were ready to learn about lousy customers. How to manage their time when dealing with them would be homework.

When the troglodyte had been able to knock down the price a decent amount, he got up from the bench and walked to a nearby vendor. Taking his wallet out halfway. The children ran after him saying it was their sale first, and were not shy in making their feelings known, to both the troglodyte and the vendor. The troglodyte told the children he didn't want to buy a good whose price wasn't firm. Stating that it must have an obvious defect. He also explained, that while they had been haggling, he had watched customers approach the vendor, buy something and leave. Allowing for the next customer's order to be filled. The troglodyte bought some chocolate from the vendor, stepped to his left and allowed the line to flow freely.

The children attacked the troglodyte. He told them there was no line behind his bench, so he wasn't comfortable giving them business. The school children left the troglodyte, cursing him in between sales to eager customers. Ones who truly wanted to help the children did so with financial contributions.

The troglodyte finished eating by the vendor, and walked around the park. He got heartburn after three laps. He lay down on a different bench. He looked up at the clear blue sky, before turning over on his side to help with the heartburn. The view wasn't as good. The view wasn't as peaceful. The panels on the bench did take his mind off the bad decision.

The troglodyte had fallen asleep on the bench and woke of his own accord, rolling over to change positions and landing on the ground. He had no problem sleeping on the ground, even if for a nap, but the force of hitting it had rung his bell. There were still a few stragglers in the park, mostly significant other couples, or families, who all seemed to have blankets.

The troglodyte didn't want to test any vendor's coffee so went elsewhere for a cup. The troglodyte entered a cafe and bought a coffee with the rest of his walking around money, taking refuge in a booth by a window. A waitress came by and started to ask if he wanted coffee, before noticing he already had it, and so didn't finish the question. The troglodyte said he did anyway. The cafe had a system where one can order a coffee ahead and bring it to a seat. Customers could also sit and order, and be serviced. If you weren't familiar with the restaurant your choice could go either way, so the cafe thought by using their system they were guaranteed to make more money. When the waitress noticed the troglodyte already had coffee, she didn't ask him if he wanted to order anything else. She didn't know why the troglodyte had said he did, when she had stopped her question short, and so forgot about him entirely as she went around to other customers asking coffee questions.

Tracing the fates of other booths in the cafe, the troglodyte saw a customer leave, and before the table could be bused, another customer take their place. A waitress saw the customer, didn't recognize they were new, there was a cup already on the table, and gave that customer the treatment. The troglodyte watched the could be customer watch the wait staff, and saw them leave without placing an order at the registers. The troglodyte left the cafe when he saw two people walking in, and placed his cup on the table of the old customer that had left.

The troglodyte walked in the dark back to his house. He didn't turn a light on when he got through the door. He knew he would have to start doing his sleeping at night. His schedule would be adjusted to accommodate the noise of the road crew. He began counting his steps, on an unusually empty stomach for when he prepared for sleep. After the rotation had been circled through, and the troglodyte had dozed off, the sun greeted him. The troglodyte knew he could get up. He rummaged around outside his house for breakfast, unfolding the canvas that had been used for a table.

From there he found some stale crackers. Cheese that was dangerously healthy. As he shook the crumbs off the canvas he heard heavy machinery drawing nearer.

The troglodyte went inside his house to grab a case of water. To offer a case to the workers. The foreman pulled up in his own truck, behind the trailers, and accepted the troglodyte's offering. The troglodyte told the foreman that loud noises disturbed the occupants of the property. They wanted the work done as fast as possible. Let the machines all run at once. The foreman said he'd do what he could but could only promise that it would get done.

The troglodyte didn't really have a problem with the noise. It was a welcome change of pace. Still, he knew that whatever wild cat was in the woods wouldn't like it, and may stay far away. He wasn't actively trying to domesticate any of the wood's wildlife, near him or afar, but once he thought it possible, he would try anything to prove it not.

The troglodyte went to his workbench and worked on a series of things to catch and capture the cat's attention. Draw it to the next trigger and so on. Hoping the cat would follow his trail of repurposed plastic, getting it used to his smell, which dominated the structure he had built. At the end of each trail would be a reward for the cat. The troglodyte planned to move the trail each time the cat took the traps, so the cat would think less of its surroundings and more of the reward. The prototypes were similar to the the plastic envelope he made. Tufts of hair were added to capture the cat's eyes. Honey smeared on the plastic for it's nose.

The troglodyte didn't want to go to the farm and send them mixed signals, so headed back down the first path. As he left his property, he saw the outline of where the road crew planned to clear and pave. They had taken all the sign posts out. The troglodyte struggled to recall where his property line was. He foresaw that it would be impeded upon. He would have to bring this up to the council before any pavement was laid, but after the path was fully cleared. If the council agreed that the road should border his property, not encroach upon, he could use the extra space for whatever he wished. If the council wouldn't budge on the road's location, he would seek restitution for the state claiming part of his land.

1⑯

The troglodyte went to where he knew the barber shop to be. He used to give them business before he sought seclusion. He tried to remember the name on the old sign while looking at the new. He walked in to the shop and said it all has to go. When the troglodyte's head was shaved he asked for the hair on the ground. A few customers helped, and pointed to spots he missed. The troglodyte was given a broom and dustpan, and kept collecting the hair. He stored it in a freezer bag that was provided. When the floor was cleaner than it had been all week, the troglodyte sealed the bag and did his best to mix up the hair. The more clumped together the hair was the better, with anything that could resemble a rodent ideal.

The troglodyte tried to pay the barber but was rejected, told he was all set and had worked off his debt. The troglodyte didn't argue and walked out, the bag of hair clutched to his chest. He didn't receive as many strange looks as he would have without the bag, and passerby from a distance thought he was holding a small pet. People that were a little closer didn't dare bother the troglodyte. They saw how tight he appeared to hold the pet. The look of determination in his eyes. When the troglodyte got back to the house he divided the hair and made twelve passable looking decoys. With hair inside each plastic covering, the troglodyte spooned honey onto the outside. Each by varying amounts. The stiff scratch sniff blast closest to where the troglodyte presumed the cat to be, would have the least amount of honey. The trap closest to the troglodyte, the most. He set three traps for a test run, and let the honey harden on the other plastic traps in wait.

The troglodyte spent the rest of the day watching the world through inside of his house. He checked on his traps through one window, the road crew and anything else happening through all the others. He tracked the machines and how they operated. Drivers would exit and could still be identified by the way they carried themself to their corresponding machine. The foreman spent his day foremost, supervising, and also watching the job through the inside of his truck. The truck was left running and the air conditioning was on. The window ever only opened to hear a question and give an answer. In that small window one has to do so.

Later in the day the foreman left the site, and returned about an hour later with his kids. The tykes ran around the job, delivering the water bottles given to the foreman that morning. After about an hour or two of that, the workers were just as tired as the kids. Everyone agreed to call it a day. When the workers had all piled into the various trucks, the ones that could leave the site, and had left, the troglodyte went out of his house to survey the damage.

They had greatly improved upon the path he had made by hand, and had made progress in the other direction as well. What they cleared didn't overlap the troglodyte's property, not very much, so he decided he wouldn't complicate matters any further with the council. If the overlap did become a point of contention, the troglodyte thought the resolution would be more swift if the project was already considered finished. This would lead to a less complicated situation for the council, there options limited, and they would most likely pay the troglodyte quickly to get rid of the headache.

The troglodyte had a fire that night. He burnt some scraps of plastic that he couldn't find any use for. The plastic changed the color of the smoke. It was thrown in frugally so the effect didn't lose its rapture. The squeal of the plastic was also entertaining, until it began to be frighten, and he had to give up on that specific repurposing task. He put the plastic out of reach and watched the fire until it needed more wood. Then he gave up on it. Enjoying it's life but not wanting to see it die. When the troglodyte was just about at his front door, the trucks with the road crew arrived at his property.

The road crew told the troglodyte what their plan for the day was. Any extra they were hoping to accomplish. They gave the troglodyte the option of painting the signs, since they now knew what the speed limit would be. The troglodyte agreed excitedly, only to feel let down, when he was given a stencil and spray paint. He thought a hand painted sign would be much more likely to get the driver's attention. He didn't compromise entirely and gradually cut pieces out of the stencil as he moved from sign to sign. The last sign had many imperfections, while the first one had few. He trimmed away at the cookie cutter design.

He threw the wet stencil in the back of the foreman's truck, so as not to disturb him, and walked as close as he was able to one of the machines actively working. Without being in danger or getting in their way. The troglodyte made a game of not being able to be seen in the operator's mirrors, and was getting pretty good, until the foreman grabbed and dragged him back to the house. The foreman was furious that the troglodyte had left the painted stencil in his truck, and with his antics around the site. Adding to the veins in the foreman's forehead, the fact that one day prior the troglodyte had said loud noises were very bad for the residents of the property. Yet here the troglodyte was, his head practically in an exhaust pipe. The troglodyte blamed his lack of sleep, sun stroke, the fumes from the spray paint, and the mania that came from seeing the foreman cool in the oasis that was his truck. Reminded of his running vehicle, the foreman left the troglodyte and returned to the air conditioning. Lucky one of his workers had a spare for the company truck.

...

The troglodyte went to the office and occupied the floor below the council's. He waited in line and swapped stories with an elderly gentleman who had been billed for something twice. The second invoice was dated a different calender year then the original. The troglodyte told the man if he were billed twice, for the job at his place, he would be furious. The troglodyte said he thought he should be the one sending out an invoice for the stress that was caused him. The elderly man couldn't agree more with the troglodyte, and confided that he worked his whole life thinking the pension he was putting in for would make life a dream. Having no other income, the pension further complicated matters with the double invoice and his taxes.

Probably having had a lifetime of conversation, the elderly man gracefully changed the subject with a joke about his own mortality. Which saved the troglodyte from having to have the last word on a dreary topic. When the elderly man went through a doorway, leaving the troglodyte alone, for the first time on that floor the troglodyte was left alone. He wasn't asked by the security what his business was. He wasn't accused of taking up space or time. The troglodyte went into the room cold when he was called. He waited until he was forced to speak, once pleasantries had silenced. The woman across from him gave no hints as to what business they conducted. The troglodyte was afraid to ask right out of the gate. He instead tried to continue the small talk, asking about the pictures she had on her desk. She shut him down, said she should be a busy woman and asked him not to be an impediment. He said he was looking for a job and hoped that he could be a busy man, a real jewel to the company. She asked for his qualifications, and not wanting to limit himself, he said he couldn't narrow them down because the company had such a broad reach. She told him to come back when he was ready to work, so the troglodyte made sure to never step foot on that floor again. He hadn't enjoyed getting past security as much as he thought he would, or having to be accountable for his being there.

The troglodyte went up one floor to wait for the council. The wait wasn't as long as the work day, which was almost done, and he saw the council members getting ready to leave. When they passed the troglodyte they were courteous. They told him they'd be back tomorrow. The troglodyte wished for them to answer what company's office was on the floor below. They couldn't help him. The troglodyte left the office shortly after the council members. He had no one to ask whether or not he should lock the doors. He went to the coffee shop.

He asked someone leaving if they were a busy body and looking for work. They didn't answer and scurried away. The troglodyte let the door close behind him and then stood in the doorway surveying the booths. He picked the cleanest one he could find and waved over one of the wait staff. He asked for a cup of coffee and a sample of the grounds that made it. When the coffee was brought to him he gave thanks and stated, this is when coffee tastes better, on the grounds that the grounds are visible. The waitress was friendly, and said food also tastes better when it is visible. The troglodyte reflected as he looked into his watery cup.

It brought up the question whether phantom taste should be considered taste, or if that was a sensation void of sense. Otherwise the waitress had been almost perfectly accurate in her statement, with the exception of the last bite on the plate. But even then there are some rare people who can appreciate the last bite. Even considering it to make the meal. When the troglodyte finished his coffee he ordered some food and told the waitress he would wait for it outside. He wanted to test whether he could taste what he ordered before it got to the booth, without the influence of smelling it being prepared. In his mind he recreated past times spent with the meal and did begin to taste how he remembered it tasting. He added hot sauce to one of his imaginary sides. His mouth started to salivate.

When the waitress called him back in for his order, he was somewhat disappointed. He had been able to taste the food while outside but had not imagined eating it in the booth where he had his coffee. He could smell his plate when the waitress opened the door and his concentration was broken by the sound of her voice. His thought experiment was ruined. He couldn't say one way or the other whether food tasted better when you could see it, and left a large tip for the help the waitress had tried to give him.

The troglodyte went back to his house. Arriving, he was glad to see the road crew had not brought lights and continued on into the night. The troglodyte knew he had to be careful with what he asked for and his hurry it up request. The troglodyte looked through the dark and guessed the work would be done within the week. The troglodyte's signs were marked where they would stand, but the troglodyte collected them and put them around his property as they had once been. He didn't put them very far in the ground, causing no trouble to the road crew save a minor inconvenience.

He walked a couple laps around the property, trying to remember all the different ways the sun shone off of the warning signs. Soon the troglodyte's eyes would be subjected to more glares than they could stand, passing cars and the cars that pass them, but at that moment there was none from the machinery on sight. The troglodyte went to his mail ditch and climbed down head first, securing his hands and feet in the slots. When he had descended the few rungs that were there, he dismounted by flipping into the mail ditch. He slept in the ditch that night, having climbed into bed.

He woke before sunrise, left the ditch and went to check on the decoys he had set up. He had no luck locating them and considered it to be a good omen. He returned to his house to grab four of the set aside traps, and brought them into the woods to set. He placed them on the ground as he'd done before, before deciding to bury them. He knew that the cat would still be able to find the traps but would have to dig out the prize, providing proof that they had been there. Allowing the troglodyte to guess at when the traps were unearthed through his very basic knowledge of carbon dating. He had watched his ditch grow in the days and weeks since he had made it, and thus was able to reasonably estimate how much time passed with a look. Variables to his guesswork included the weather and other wildlife, but if the troglodyte was vigilant he could uncover the cat's eating patterns. He assumed the cat would only scavenge for the honey traps once they had already hunted, learning from their last outing that the clumps of hair had no center, and so would not be too tempted by the sight of them.

When the troglodyte had his four holes dug, he gave each trap a home and buried them. The troglodyte walked out of the woods and saw the road crew at work. He walked to the nearest piece of heavy machinery, and standing in one spot, watched the operator until they thought the troglodyte wanted to talk to them. They idled the equipment. When the operator had closed the distance to the troglodyte, they asked if he could be helped. The troglodyte said he hoped so and walked past the operator to their machine. He climbed into it and yelled to the operator outside, asking what he should do first. The operator was offended, so told the troglodyte the first thing he needed to do was take a safety class. The troglodyte was crestfallen, knew the operator's words were true, and gave the reins back. The operator said where they had taken the class, and that there were countless rhymes and slogans to learn so they'd be safe on the job. The troglodyte was then subjected to many of the slogans. The last he heard as he walked away was, 'if machine light flashing, chance of crashing; if hear it beeps, look out for creeps.'

The troglodyte walked to the hub of the construction site, the foreman's truck, and eventually persuaded him to roll down the window. It took incessant tapping on the glass. The window rolled down enough to show the foreman's eyes, but nothing below that. The foreman tried to say something. The troglodyte couldn't hear him over the sound of the air conditioning in the truck. He was unable to read his lips. The troglodyte disregarded whatever the foreman was trying to say, and asked him how many days his crew had went without an accident. The foreman gave their number, then the tally for the current job site. The troglodyte asked if there was anything he could do to help secure the site. The foreman said he had a few ideas and tried to wait out the troglodyte. The troglodyte sensed the conversation was over and motioned with his hand rolling up a car window, to let the foreman know he conceded. The troglodyte walked past the truck bed, seeing the outline of where the stencil had been, and headed in the direction of town.

1⑦

He made it to the bait and tackle garage and was met with a smile by his acquaintance. The troglodyte said he was looking for a way to fish without a fishing pole. The seller said he had nets that could be used, but the troglodyte was not interested in buying anything. He admitted he could have been clearer with his original question. The man said there were people who could harvest the river using only their hands. He didn't know the technique, but made quite a seller's argument for all the ways a fishing line has improved on that design. He further tried to push his wares. The conversation came to a head and they to an agreement. The troglodyte could borrow the pole. Any fish he caught could be redeemed and used as payment for the rental. If the fish were biting, the troglodyte caught could trade in for ownership of the pole or any other equipment he might need. Provided the fish longed to be on the hook for something.

The troglodyte asked what bait he should use. He didn't know that depended on what he wanted to catch. The seller said the more expensive lures or bait could catch more valuable fish, but the troglodyte would have to provide extra fish in order to rent out the added equipment. The troglodyte decided serving worms would be fine, didn't like the price the seller offered for them, and headed up the river.

When the troglodyte found a shady spot to sit, that might be a suitable place to fish, he began unearthing rocks. Digging around him to find worms. He thought he found more than he did and didn't notice at first that a few of the worms had very short legs. When he was ready to fish, he tied three crawlers together, put them on the hook and cast his line. When the troglodyte returned to the garage at dusk he had with him four fish. Fish which had been sitting out in the sun for the greater part of the day. The seller said he would only be able to use the fish as stock, but that even with their decreased value, the troglodyte still offered a fair exchange. The fish the troglodyte brought covered his use of the fishing pole. Also the loss the seller faced while the pole was not in his shop. The seller gave the troglodyte store credit. Next time he wanted to fish it would be free of surcharge. If the troglodyte were to catch more fish during his free outing, he may be able to trade and keep the fishing pole permanently. Keeping the fish on ice would require a cooler, which the troglodyte could also borrow for a price. Or, the troglodyte could exchange the fish out of water as stock, again, for decreased value.

When the seller and troglodyte were just about done finalizing the terms of their pseudo contract, a customer walked in. The customer interrupted the seller, damn near in the middle of his speech, to ask about some obscure lure. The seller was delighted the potential customer was familiar with the product. He offered an outstretched hand to the troglodyte so that they could finalize a deal, and he would be free to help a fellow enthusiast. The troglodyte accepted and stayed around the garage for a glimpse of the reverent lure. The troglodyte didn't get the chance to see it, was asked to leave, and the garage door was closed behind him. The troglodyte wondered what this added measure did for the security of the marketplace, but resisted the urge to lift the garage door to find out. Opening the lid of that tuna can would release the fishy odor back into the world, and it having been marinating since the troglodyte's trade, he hoped for the sake of the seller's neighbors that the transaction wouldn't take too long.

The troglodyte stayed in the neighborhood, asking anyone he passed about the bait and tackle business. He was met with the same answer from the many people he questioned, who said you can't see the nose on your own face, then pointed in the direction of the garage. The troglodyte told these people he wanted a commoner's opinion and that he distrusted renowned experts. None of the people were willing to denounce themselves, all thinking themself expert in some field or distinction, and took offense to the troglodyte. Once the people the troglodyte had been questioning started to walk away, and without fail start conversations with the next person they saw, the troglodyte knew it was time to leave. He exited the bait and tackle neighborhood, returning to the center of the town in the dark.

...

The troglodyte went to the bar in town and stood across from the barkeep, who was busy pouring sand. The troglodyte observed the responsible, the lightweights and the heavy drinkers. There is a subset of heavy drinkers that want everyone around to see the edge of the world with them. They will try to goad the responsible ones into playing their game but it is usually the lightweights who succumb. The lightweights are able to see what the heavy drinkers cannot, so the heavy drinkers stay close to them.

The bar was lined with the mugs of all three groups and the bartender had someone on his shoulders changing a light bulb, so that nothing would be knocked over. When the bulb was changed and the helper had dismounted, the bartender told the troglodyte he sometimes needed help to keep the lights on. He asked for his order. The troglodyte said he'd take a soda and a table, and was led to one of those islands for the sober of mind.

People at the bar were balancing stacks of quarters on their elbows, before trying to catch the stack with their hand. Successful attempts brought about cheers from onlookers, who provided more quarters to the pot. One participant was thrown out of the bar after he was found to be adding coins, which resembled quarters in all but weight, with each hand he won. He would pocket the quarters from the last attempt, and retrieve from a separate pocket the fakes. He was discovered after he bowed out of the competition but was still throwing in for the pot. Upon counting out their hand, one of the players noticed the fakes. Which led to the emptying out of all pockets onto the bar. The forger was taken for all they had and escorted out of the bar to look for the next good game.

The troglodyte took the forger's spot at the bar, and got a good look at the contents of all the bar-goer's pockets. As the people at the bar stuffed their pockets, they were reminded that there was more to do than watch themselves bring their hands to their mouth. Many left. Those were the responsible drinkers who were staying true to their namesake, rousing some of the lightweights to leave with them. The heavy drinkers, and those building up their tolerance, stayed around and had plenty of questions for the troglodyte. His drink was a different color than theirs and he didn't seem as weighed down.

When the bartender announced last call, the troglodyte bought a beer for the road and took it back to his house. He opened the tab and rearranged some of the stuff in the fridge, so that he wouldn't forget the can when he needed it. He closed the fridge and tied a knot around the handles, so he wouldn't forget to check the fridge, to remind himself what it was he would need to remember. He then went back to the spot he had found the string to tie the knot, and placed one of his non perishables there. He didn't keep any non perishables in the fridge, but hoped he would think the product out of place, return it to where it belonged, notice the missing string, and investigate further. With this done he went to his bed and slept atop the covers, so that when he woke up he would have to wonder why he did so.

When the troglodyte woke, he only wondered why he couldn't sleep as well every time, and got ready for the day. He put on his uniform and racked his brain for any examples of shirts with a breast pocket on the opposite side. Not being able to recall ever seeing any, he put his shirt inside out, before securing money by means of a paper clip attached to the pocket. He went out the back door of his house, thinking it was his front because of the location of the road crew. He was impressed with their progress and wondered if his neighbors were receiving the same level of attention. He headed down the second path and to the farm, not minding the thought of being disturbed, so long as it was on his own terms.

He saw the other town's handiwork before seeing any of their workers. The other town had started where the foreman and the crew the troglodyte knew, would finish, and were working their way toward the farm. When the farmer answered the door he was angry with the troglodyte, recognizing him as the messenger, and accused him of hurting his business. The farmer had postponed his plans for a week, expecting a road crew to arrive and interrupt what business he had to take care of. Having not yet seen the road crew and his output stagnant, the farmer didn't know what to believe. He found believing anything difficult, so when the troglodyte told him the crew was more than half done, he was still thinking about looking for another job.

The farmer invited the troglodyte in, he was also without a schedule, and offered the troglodyte refreshments. The troglodyte accepted and soon they were talking about caring for animals. The troglodyte segued into the tracking and trapping of wildlife, in order that the domesticated be cared for, but wasn't able to find the farmer's thoughts useful. When the conversation finished, the troglodyte asked the farmer for any wool he might have. The troglodyte was given a few bags, full of the stuff. The farmer didn't ask what the troglodyte was going to use it for. He hoped it wasn't for some malevolent form of tar and feather revenge, which he thought would have been taking it too far, and he himself wouldn't choose to do if the road crew ever arrived at his property.

The troglodyte continued on to the center of the farmer's town. This town's people thought he was carrying pillows, rather than a small pet. He spent some time sitting on the curb of a pedestrian street, taking his chances with getting hit by a bicycle instead of a car. His knees were almost in his chest, the bags of wool pressed between, and he was extremely comfortable. People that passed him in that position asked where the troglodyte developed such a posture. He told them it came from a farm. He was approached by workout clothes wielders and dirty looking people in sandals, who wanted to hear his thoughts. Dogs barked at him instinctively from far away.

When the troglodyte felt sufficiently rested, he borrowed a phone from a person he had shared words with, and asked them for the number of a hack. They called one for him and handed over their phone. When the hack showed up it kept some distance from the troglodyte, before driving off. The troglodyte borrowed the same phone, redialed the last call and said one of their cars had just driven off on him. The dispatcher asked for his location, then told the troglodyte to wait at the street's end. A car would be there for him shortly. Within minutes of being dispatched, a hack pulled up and waited in the designated area. This time the troglodyte went to it and found transport back to the town. When the hack ride ended the troglodyte reached into his shirt and paid the driver.

1⑧

The troglodyte went to the couple's house and found them both there. They invited the troglodyte in, asking what was new in his neck of the woods. He told them the road was nearly finished. The one that connected the town to his house, and his house to the other town, by way of the farm. They congratulated the troglodyte on his good fortune. They showed him to their garage, where they implored him to take a bicycle. Free of charge. The couple figured the troglodyte could make better use of it than themselves, and explained all the faults and defects of the bike. They had the troglodyte take the bike out of the garage and coached him as he practiced riding down the street. When the troglodyte was able to navigate on his own, he thanked them for their good will and told them to visit him soon if they were passing through.

The troglodyte rode back in the direction of his house, making sure to push down on the right pedal extra hard when it came back to the top, easing up during it's ascent. When the couple's house was no longer visible, the troglodyte happened across fellow cyclists, going at a marginally faster clip than him. He did his best to keep up, wasn't able to, but saw the bike path the cyclists were heading to. He then lessened his pace, saving his energy for the bike trail in case he would have to pedal all the way back.

To all the people he passed on the trail he gave fair warning. If he moved by them on the left or right he said so, those in front of him he yelled he was coming in hot. The passerby were good at adhering to the troglodyte's warnings and there were no accidents that day. Trails led off of the bike path to picnic tables that were being used. The troglodyte was invited over to one, after standing awkwardly over his bike nearby. The family of four had a pretty good spread but assured the troglodyte it would go to waste if he didn't join them. The troglodyte refused to say no. If not for the sake of himself or the family, then at least for the food. Whose whole life lead to that moment and he didn't wish it purgatory.

The food would be discarded. Where it would wait for a meal never to come. With full knowledge of why a meal is, but not what it is. So the troglodyte joined the family and made sure not to leave a single morsel on his plate, or any that he had access to. The family asked whatever questions came to mind while the troglodyte chewed, and expected clear concise answers when he was between mouthfuls. Each member of the family had their own line of questioning, with the questions made in a round, so that person b's question followed person a's, and person a followed person d. At first when the questions started, the troglodyte needed to be quick on his feet to provide an answer. Once he discovered the pattern, he was able to easily shift between topics because he knew which subject would be brought up next. When the picnic was over the troglodyte asked his only question. He got four different answers. None that would be helpful on their own, but together provided the troglodyte with something coherent.

The troglodyte continued on the bike trail, heading further from the couple's house, until he came to a fork in the path. The troglodyte took the right path and circled back to the left path before going back in the direction he came. He passed the family, who were now washing their dinnerware in a still pool of water. They waved to the troglodyte, splashing drops of water on to their face. The troglodyte waved back, smiling at first before turning stone

faced. He was unsure of his rapport with them, and didn't
know whether to laugh at their slight misfortune or
sympathize.

When he got near the beginning end, he exited the trail,
and had to adjust his way of riding the bike for the new old
terrain. He had no destination in mind, so rode through the
town familiarizing himself with easy and difficult routes, for
this mode of travel. After cruising the streets for a few hours,
the troglodyte went to a gas station. He leaned his bike
against one of the pumps.

He went into the store and bought a tourist's map of the
town. As well as a few different colored markers. He moved
down the counter after he paid, across from an empty register,
and outlined different routes he could take the bike on. If the
bike was under performing or various weather conditions
were a factor, he wouldn't have to wonder what if, and
would be able to course correct. The map also provided a
good insurance policy for if his bike were ever stolen.
Assuming the bike was stolen to be ridden, not thrown in the
back of a vehicle, the troglodyte could follow the map and
likely find the thief struggling to get the bike to move along
some of the more difficult routes. The troglodyte put the
markers into his shirt and rode back to his property.

The troglodyte flushed his body with water when he got
into the house, and had three non perishables, high in protein,
for his aching muscles. He stowed the bike against one of the
walls, handlebars on the floor with rear tire in the air, and
went to track down the road crew. When he found them and
saw half of the crew already had left, the troglodyte knew
they had finished the job. Had the other town's road crew
started at the farm house, the troglodyte wouldn't have been
able to make his assumption as easily. He saw the worker

who told him safety was important, and congratulated them on a job well done. The worker told the troglodyte they couldn't have done it without him, the distractions provided allowed for work to be resumed with even greater focus. The troglodyte was happy to have helped, and felt even better than that for doing so without the knowledge he was at the time.

The troglodyte took the revelation over to the foreman. He told him he was welcome for what had been done. The foreman told him the signs looked great, although it appeared the troglodyte didn't have the steadiest of hands. The foreman suggested he have his hands looked at. The troglodyte had expected a more profound thanks giving, and tried to persuade the foreman to flatter him some more. The foreman said that seeing the troglodyte's house all alone in the woods, and never having seen the other occupants, inspired in the workers diligence. They wanted to get it over with and go home to see their familiars. The troglodyte took the compliment how he wanted to and took his chips off the table. He asked the foreman if he knew when the other road crew would finish. He was told they already had.

Apparently the farmer couldn't wait any longer to be back in the farm league, and had had the road crew stop in their tracks. Leaving the rest unpaved. At that section the speed limit would change, so as to not destroy tires and undersides of vehicles. The foreman informed the troglodyte that the paint on the signs of the other side of the road would need to be removed. They were to be coated with the correct information. The foreman said it would be a thankless job, since the other road crew had already left the site, as had his team, but it had to get done. The troglodyte took the job. He told the foreman he would make him proud. When asked to explain, the troglodyte said that if he were questioned while repainting the signs, he would say foreman's orders. The questioner would think the foreman a great man for thinking of driver's safety and the integrity of their vehicles.

The foreman didn't follow the troglodyte's logic. He thought the only reason anyone would question the troglodyte working would be because someone was clearly unhappy with what he was doing. The troglodyte dropping the foreman's name could only soil his reputation. The foreman didn't voice these thoughts, and instead told the troglodyte he couldn't be more proud and that the troglodyte was one of a kind. As the foreman drove off and the troglodyte wandered down the road, both were glad with who they were and grateful to not have to switch positions. They said as much when they parted, though only jokingly.

The troglodyte made quick work repainting the signs and didn't make any alterations to the stencil. He was more concerned that people follow the speed limit near his house, and thought the signs he was currently working on somewhat pointless. Since cars would be approaching or driving away from a farm, the troglodyte thought that animal crossing signs might have served a better purpose. He had no one to bitch and moan to. No one to play the wrong tree. So instead worked angrily, which it not being a job involving finesse, worked to his advantage. When all the signs had been changed and were yet to be dented from rocks right as rain, the troglodyte returned to his house.

Undoing the knot from the refrigerator door, he got the opened beer he had been saving. His original plan slightly altered, he got down his bicycle from the wall and walked it to where the start of the path he made had been. He mounted the bicycle and rode the length of the road. Spilling small amounts from his cup, the can, as he went.

This was how he anointed the road. He hoped that his superstition may save any possible drunk drivers. If there was already booze on the road, and there was some also in the driver's system, perhaps they might find safer passage because of the connection. However, what was in the system may want to join what was on the road, which would be disastrous. The troglodyte hoped for the former outcome, but, as with any superstition, knew nothing may happen at all.

When his beer can was empty, he found himself on the farmer's property. He kicked the bike stand out and tossed the can into one of the fields where cows were grazing. The farm hand the troglodyte met on his first visit would later find the can. The farm hand will then walk with the can in hand, searching for a way to dispose of it properly. From there they are interrogated by the farmer. All roads lead to accusations of drinking on the job, so the farm hand loses his occupational patronym and becomes despondent. Whether the farm hand saw more or less faces after he was fired is unknown. He did run into the troglodyte once near a coffee machine. There he relayed his story.

It took the troglodyte about a quarter of the time to bike the road as it would have taken him to walk it, provided there was no traffic. If a car passed him while on his bike, he would stop and wait for it to go by. Whereas if he was walking, he could continue without stopping, as long as he stayed in the gutter. On days when there was a lot of traffic the troglodyte usually chose to walk. His bike could prove difficult to start riding again after completely stopped. He began to recognize certain cars on the road and became familiar with their schedules, which became his schedule if he saw them on a number of consecutive days. The troglodyte even learned how to distinguish angry beeps from friendly honks, and how he would respond accordingly.

If they were light on the horn with a couple honks, he would usually throw his hand in the air to wave, without looking at who was acknowledging him. If the driver beeped loud and long, the troglodyte would dive to his right, getting off the road as quickly as possible. The jumping away was more about giving the driver something to think about, rather than for the troglodyte's own safety. If he didn't get hit in the post office parking lot, he wouldn't get hit now. If the driver saw such a severe reaction from the troglodyte because of their laying on the horn, maybe next time they would think twice before trying to outmanoeuvre him.

The troglodyte didn't get hurt abandoning his bike or leaving his feet. Not after the first few times. He developed muscle memory for how to fall, and his body learned to take the impact. His passive aggressive plan backfired when the friendly honks began to turn into aggressive beeps. All wanted to see the spectacle of the fearful pedestrian. Angry beepers started to take advantage, passing the troglodyte multiple times in a day. Some drivers would even partner together so that one car would pass the troglodyte and throw something out the window, while another passed honking their horn. They hoped the troglodyte would jump right in to the newly put down trash. When the troglodyte had started to camouflage, he stopped using the road for recreation and decided to only make use of it when he had somewhere he needed to go.

1⑨

The troglodyte was surprised to find his first piece of mail when he checked the chute. It was addressed to his residence, titled to a whom, whom it may concern. He opened the letter languidly and found an invitation for the grand reopening of the buffet. It stated the restaurant had been closed for renovation, but now offered a better dining experience. Claims of a satiation sensation. Nowhere in the letter was mention of any recent legal troubles the owners may have had.

The story of the child was just as believable as any remodeling done, so the troglodyte decided to go to the opening, so he may uncover the truth. He was in luck that the date was set for that night, but supposed he wouldn't have checked for mail if this wasn't the case. And when he did get around to checking the mail there probably wouldn't have been that invitation, though a different one for a fast approaching date may have been there.

The troglodyte took his bike to the restaurant and was force fed both sides of the story. There were people formed in a line, on the restaurants side, who didn't mind the wait because they knew the experience inside would make it all worthwhile. There were other people chanting in a crowd and holding signs, protesting. The chant was, 'fine print, here's a splint, between the lines, should be fine.' With signs that read 'all you can eat, must be neat' and 'endless meal, so too ordeal.'

Trying their best to keep both parties at bay were restaurant staff, out of practice handling disgruntled customers, mostly because of their time off. Some of the new hires began to be persuaded by the protesters. They were relieved of their duty once spotted and told to help prep food inside. As the line grew longer and more people joined the crowd in protest, it became too much for the restaurant staff to handle. The authorities were called. When they showed up, both pregamed parties found that the enemy of their enemy was their friend, for a little while, until constables began to show bias to one side or the other. Then both the protesters and the people in line joined together to fight for their right to loiter. Soon the front of the restaurant was clear of any people. Some signs that they had been were still there.

The people, though dispersed, had still heard the message that was shouted over all the commotion. The reopening would be pushed back three days, and they hoped to see all the faces of their happy customers then. The troglodyte left the restaurant without any new information on the disappearance of the buffet, and followed the now mixed crowd into an open eatery. The crowd, having just been at each other's throats, were now more concerned with their own and ate very well. The troglodyte ate up their camaraderie and listened as they reminisced about insults they used on the constables. Hearing this, the troglodyte truly couldn't tell which side the people gathered at the table were on, the signs thrown about them giving no clues. He thought the protester's insults would have stood out easily, but the people who had been in line proved to be just as cunning in their meanness. When the table had finished with the main course, a waiter asked if dessert should be brought out. The troglodyte said just keep them coming and left. As he exited the restaurant he heard the argument resume over the buffet. He didn't turn around to see which faces belonged to which cause.

The troglodyte hadn't ordered anything at the restaurant besides a suggestion for dessert, so he used his money to buy a couple hours from a motel. It wouldn't be the cleanest place to sleep, but he hadn't been around the town's folk enough to have any idea of the kind of people that might use the rooms. He didn't worry. He sat on the bed for a couple minutes and surveyed the room he was in. He used his shirt as a cover for the pillow, less because of concern for his hygiene and more because he couldn't stand it's smell, and went to sleep.

He woke to a phone call telling him his time in the motel was almost up. He could add more by dialing a code or going to the front desk. The troglodyte didn't like the idea of being woken up violently a second time, so decided he was well enough rested to leave the room. He put his shirt back where it belonged, he needed as much help as he could get, and went to a spot where he could set and think.

The troglodyte didn't sleep on any of the benches in the park nor did he disturb anyone stargazing. He sat and tried to see into the darkness as far as he could. It was slow progress he made adjusting his vision. If he broke his concentration he'd have to start over. If his eyes lingered on a spot for too long he lost the ability to see the pattern of the empty black space void of detailed objects, because of impeding dark spots. He had to blink, and constantly move his eyes from some point and immediately back. Since the horizon is as it is, no matter how far the troglodyte tried to look, there was always more darkness beyond his point of reference. He could push the darkness back to an extent, but would need to repeat the process shortly thereafter.

He got a headache trying to expand how far he could see. He still kept up with the practice until day broke, to see if a sunrise could be a common cure. After the sun had risen, and enough time had passed that his headache was no more, the troglodyte closed his eyes and made a realization. Just as he was able to push the darkness away, it also was able to push back. If he had attempted to fix his vision in the hours leading up to the middle of the night his point of reference would have been deceptively close. So if the troglodyte had just watched the sunrise he could have spent his time on the bench a different way and saved himself a headache.

...

The troglodyte ran into a man who already had a headache, though the sun had just rose. He was the owner of one of the gas stations in town, and was trying to get a license to sell tobacco. It didn't matter how much he lowered the price of gasoline, he hardly had any foot traffic through his store. He said his competitors had people bumping shoulders down the aisles. He said the reason he couldn't get a license was because the town was asking too much from him in taxes. The troglodyte thought taxes could only be collected if money was made off the tobacco, and said something to that extent. He prophesied if the tobacco was kept behind glass, showing no intent to distribute, the owner could increase foot traffic without incurring penalty.

The question was whether or not the store owner was willing to give up space on his shelves for a product that wouldn't sell. The store owner offered the troglodyte free choice of anything on the shelves around him, telling him he had to start making space, and whatever the troglodyte wanted to take was well deserved. The troglodyte grabbed a couple packs of lighters, some cases of water and a box of trash bags. He reinforced the trash bags so they wouldn't break and he could walk carefree, with the bag over his shoulder, unconcerned with the weight of his spoils. He told a couple people on the street that the gas station nearby would soon start selling smokes. The people believed him, judging from his appearance that he'd be the type to know.

The troglodyte then went to the other competitive gas station, and searched for the cases of water, lighters and trash bags. Nowhere around any of those items could the troglodyte see tobacco, so figured his beneficiary to be in good shape. He didn't buy anything in the gas station, but was conscious there were eyes on him. Those eyes probably told their brains to wonder if a shirt was in the bag that the troglodyte might be able to wear right side out.

The troglodyte brought his prize back to his property. He walked through the woods so he wouldn't have to continue the game of, cars on the road. Still without reason not to be superstitious, the troglodyte didn't want to disappoint the drivers, there was yet to be an accident on the new road, and so didn't pay to play. The troglodyte hadn't paid attention to the road at night, and couldn't be sure how his other blessing fared.

When he got to his house he stacked the new water next to the old, then put the old cases on the new stack. He put the lighters in storage near the workbench. He got all the air he could out of the trash bags he used, licked their respective seams, and put them back in the box. He put the box of trash bags near the door to the back of his house, and went to the front of his house to resume transcribing his notes. He sat on one of the chairs that was less piled on to than the others, and used his leg for a table. The last note he had written down was, a few eggs were broken to make the omelet, but a few omelets were made to to be broken. He copied from there on. He stopped for the night with, Serene, she watched the sun set. Only able for she knew it set to rise.

The troglodyte spent the morning preparing more traps for the wild cat to follow, using wool where he had hair before. He brought the traps with him to the woods. He didn't set any until he checked on those already all set. The troglodyte guessed by the look of the lightly caked holes, that the cat had dug up the honey scented plastic disposable very soon after they were put down. The troglodyte checked his new traps later that day.

When he found the fourth trap dug up but the fifth one still untouched, he knew the cat must be nearby, and stood still. His eyes focused as if he was looking at a picture. When his mind started to wander and his eyes wished to focus on something, he forced himself to zone out so he'd be able to detect movement easier. The troglodyte was told, motion on his right, but fought all urges to move his head to have a better look, and remained completely still. He heard no accompanying foot steps with the shadow, no hints as to whether the cat was approaching or receding. When the troglodyte believed it was safe to move, he did so, and was successful.

He left the woods, determined to keep setting traps, though now with a different objective in mind. He, himself, had felt trapped when he was out in the woods, and didn't wish to return the feeling to the cat who had been his oppressor. Instead, he would set the trash canisters as a token of his appreciation for being spared. They would be his way of communicating his thoughts about a free lunch. The troglodyte stopped leaving the traps one day, after seeing bark peeled off a nearby tree where he was setting.

When the troglodyte discovered something was trying to butt in on his relationship with the cat, he dismantled the traps and took the wool out of any unused canisters. He thought the best way to move forward would be to get rid of the wool and repurpose the plastic. He knew he couldn't give up the honey, and was ready to face the challenge of being reminded what could have been with every spoonful. He used the plastic to make a sort of sculpture. Two water bottles were put together, the body, and, two bottles halved, the legs. He covered the sculpture with wool, using some honey for an adhesive.

His creation had no eyes. It had no features of any kind. What it had going for it it was, if a viewer was told what it was supposed to be, they may be able to see some resemblance in the abstraction. It could have been a Ouessant lamb. The troglodyte brought the doll as far into the woods as he dared, and left it for the cat. His thinking was that even if they couldn't be together, the cat could at least have something to remember him by. He knew that some primates cared for dolls of humans as if they were their own, and half hoped the wild cat might do the same with his baby.

The troglodyte left the woods and his property on foot, and headed to the office. When he got to the floor of the council, he stopped by the secretary's desk to chat. The secretary thanked the troglodyte for hosting, before taking issue with his caterers. They had come to her house one Saturday morning, preaching about all types of things, never letting the secretary get a word in. When she finally told them she wasn't interested, they asked for their dinnerware and said they were sent by the troglodyte. The secretary couldn't believe representatives of a restaurant would be so in her face, spouting their personal views.

The troglodyte didn't correct the secretary, that they were church goers who cant think of food without talking, and asked if she did give them their dinnerware back. She had, but said when she went into her house to get it the two women followed her in. They asked for refreshments and to be accommodated, so the secretary prepared a plate of food for them and got them drinks. When the church women had picked around the plate and were ready to leave, they asked for their stuff. They checked to make sure it was all there. It wasn't. There was a plate missing. They missed the plate right in front of them. The secretary only noticed it later, when she cleared it, and had time to do the dishes. The secretary had no plans to return the plate, and paid the women before they left so she wouldn't have to associate with them again.

...

The troglodyte left the secretary to wait in line for the council. When the council saw him in, the troglodyte demanded he be paid for the land given up for their road. Since the troglodyte's property didn't fall under their jurisdiction, the council said they were unable to help him. They did tell him however, that they had come to an agreement with the other town. The road was in the process of becoming a toll road. The take would be divided between both towns. There would be a booth built just outside of the troglodyte's property. Another booth built in the vicinity of the farm.

The troglodyte asked for whose benefit the tolls were being enacted. The response he got was, a child eats for their parent's benefit, without knowing they're doing it for themselves. The tolls would make the town seem selfish, but in truth the drivers would be the most positively impacted. The council said the troglodyte had left them no choice. When he decided to reintroduce himself to society, he had asked to be accommodated, and the initial construction of the road could only have lead to future projects. The council said they would notify the troglodyte by mail if there were to be any more new projects, so that there would be no more surprised outrage the next time they met. They would provide notice if he needed to get his thoughts in order.

Construction would begin the next day, with tolls collected a week from then. The road could be used toll free up to that point, whether the booths were finished early or an attendant was inside. The troglodyte left the council and hoped he would be able to host them again, despite the newly added expense of doing so.

If the council wanted to visit the troglodyte again they would have to walk, as they had the first time, or take the toll road. With the latter, they would need to find a place to get off before they could start walking. The road went straight past the troglodyte's house, with no driveway to connect to or exits for circling back. The troglodyte wondered how long it would be before he saw those changes as well.

He went back to his house to begin working on repurposing plastic, so that it could easily hold and disperse coins. He gutted a water bottle before rolling one side under the other, and drove his needle through to force it to maintain his desired shape. He made four differently sized plastic cigars, for the varying widths of the coins, and repeated the process over. These would be his gifts for the toll booth attendants. They would bring his neighbor count up to three. He hoped that the attendants would bring their own lunches. He didn't want to be disturbed while trying not to have his.

He wondered if there were rules about what was appropriate to bring to lunch. Perhaps there were even more if the workplace is in such a confined space. Just as the lure salesman reopening his garage after a high interest sale, the toll booth must surely reek when the window is slid open. Maybe that was why people paid with exact change, to save themself from not one minor inconvenience but many. He put the water bottle caps on the bottom of the new coin collectors and worked on finding a way to allow the right amount of coins to be dropped into the hand. He settled on putting a cap on the top, only one coin could be dispensed at a time if there was any concern with accuracy, and fastened it as he had the lower cap. If the teller needed to have two or more coins they would flip the carrier over after pulling the tab, pull the other tab, and repeat the process as necessary.

The troglodyte then took all the unused plastic he had, which was plastic that had already been used but now had no purpose, and cut away whatever flat pieces were there. Most of the rounded pieces he weighed down, but a few he put aside. He got his lighter and began fusing the flat pieces of plastic together, until he had two patchwork squares that were each about the size of his torso. He used the rounded pieces to secure his two squares together, leaving a hole in the middle of his design. When the plastic had sufficiently cooled he put the vest on and went outside.

He didn't walk in the gutter of the new road, not wanting to test the durability of his vest just yet, and instead walked in the woods. In the opposite direction of where he left the doll with his cat. He didn't swing his arms as he walked, already exhibiting chafing from the plastic, and sort of resembled a floating water cooler. There were a few people on the beach, and asked what he was promoting when they saw him. The troglodyte didn't have a cause for their concern and was unable to provide them satisfactory answers.

A couple people thought out loud what the troglodyte might represent when his responses fell flat.

Someone posed that since man is an island, maybe he portrayed the trash islands out at sea. Another said they were reminded more of a landfill, as the collection there has legs. The troglodyte wasn't offended by their observations, even doing his best to prove them both right, by walking up to the water and going in. He was helped to float by his preserver. When the troglodyte returned from the water he was asked if he accepted donations, which he said he did, but that he didn't have the proper channels to make their contributions count. Because of the troglodyte's selfless act that day, the two people who had an eye for design teamed up, to make sure that proper channels were established to fund the aforementioned causes. After the plastic and clothes that were set out had dried, the troglodyte followed the road leading away from the lake, carrying the vest on his shoulders.

The troglodyte walked to where he could find the constabulary, still carrying his plastic, and asked when the next ride along would be. The constable at the front desk said he had just missed it, since none on patrol saw him carrying the strange object. The troglodyte explained the vest away. The constable transcribed his description, adding some numbers, **/**, to the end of the note. He then brought up a screen with all the constables on patrol in the area, and told the troglodyte he may have to wait a while.

The troglodyte took a seat near the entrance of the station, and used one of the desk tables that accompanied each chair. The tables were bolted down so the chairs wouldn't have to be. The troglodyte made use of both of his hands, desperately trying to balance the plastic vest. He was saved from his adversary when a constable interrupted, telling him the ride was there. The troglodyte got out of his seat, joints cracking because of the tension built up in his body, and followed the constable out of the station.

The constable's car was still running when they approached. The troglodyte was glad to see the front windows were down. The constable told the troglodyte he could put the cone for his dog in the back, but the troglodyte said he'd feel safer having it up front. They drove off responding to a call. The troglodyte used the constable's suggestion, placing the vest upside down on his head, when he found the noise and lights too alarming. The constable gave up on the troglodyte's explanation once his voice became muffled, and drove with his eyes on the road, neither turning to look at any confused drivers or the passenger to his right.

When they got to the scene and the constable had shut off the sirens, the troglodyte removed the plastic from his head and reached for the door handle. The constable stopped him, telling him he had to stay in the car because they were first to arrive. He wasn't sure of the danger yet. The constable reached under his seat, put on a bullet proof vest then jacket over top. The troglodyte said if he went with the constable the threat level may greatly be reduced. The constable said by adding any extra bodies the threat level would always increase, because another person would be put in danger. The troglodyte pleaded his case for what felt like minutes to the constable, before the constable gave him permission to be a colleague for the day.

He gave the troglodyte a jacket and told him to wear it over his plastic poncho, and not say anything while they responded to the call. They exited the vehicle and the troglodyte began walking a little too eagerly towards the house. He had to keep being told to slow down and walk with the constable, not ahead of him. The constable knocked on the door while he had the troglodyte ring the doorbell, explaining that this alerted the residents there was more than one constable on the scene. The troglodyte suggested he knock on a window, so as to be out of reach of the doorbell, which would confirm their numbers. When the constable was going back down the steps so he could rap on a window, the door opened, so he turned around to cover the troglodyte.

The woman who opened the door said tactfully that she was the caller, when she saw the troglodyte and the constable tactically switch positions, dissuading them from any played out antics. The constable asked what the problem was, to which the woman replied that someone had been going through her trash on days she left it outside. The constable asked for any proof that the culprit was a human and not an animal scavenging, and getting none, gave her the number for animal control. The woman demanded more from the constables, but backed down when the troglodyte repeated the constable's first question, playing the bad stereotype. She thanked them for their time. Walking back to the car it was the constable who was brisk, practically running so he could yell at the troglodyte once they were both back inside. The troglodyte didn't understand why the constable was mad, since he hadn't said anything the constable himself wouldn't have said. The constable explained that once he gave out the number to another department, he essentially excused himself from the call. The troglodyte's antics could have roped them right back in. The troglodyte took off the jacket upon hearing this, deciding that he'd stay in the car for any of the other calls.

Later in the day, the constable dropped the troglodyte back off at the station and continued on his patrol. The troglodyte went inside and told the constable, who didn't make desks and just sat in one, that he wouldn't be going on any more ride alongs. The constable asked him if there was a problem, and the troglodyte spun on his heels. He got in one of the hacks nearby, one that was not too shabby but not too nice, so he knew the driver wouldn't be expecting a big tip, and asked how far he could go with what money he had. The driver told him the destination, then turned on talk radio.

The topic that was being discussed was relevant to the driver's profession, but not that driver specifically. One of the hosts said that sitting in traffic should be considered time on the clock, while the other debated him on the subject. Her view was that time spent sitting in traffic was to be factored in to the paycheck they received, and since the paycheck wasn't used on the clock, the time spent when they could use their paycheck should not be considered business hours. If someone were to sit in traffic and make a personal purchase, they should be able to do so without facing repercussion from the company they worked for. If they were on the clock and completed an order, they would have to be held to higher standards. One of the hosts just wasn't comfortable with that.

The other host believed that when someone is sitting in traffic their mind can stray, but will inevitably return back to thoughts of business. Thus they should be compensated accordingly. Even if the employee is heading home from work, the added time in traffic will allow for productive thoughts, and if these thoughts were to wander, turning angry, the employee may wish to do them justice and resume them while at home. The hack driver pulled into the post office parking lot and told the troglodyte that was as far as she could take him. When the troglodyte asked why she had chose the post office and not a different place of similar distance, the hack driver said that she was able to wait in that lot for as long as was needed, without getting a ticket. The troglodyte wondered if the loss of fares would outweigh the fines, but saw his seat was taken shortly after he left the car.

The troglodyte went into the post office and checked for any mail. He broke the sticker placed over his locker and found a small book inside. He opened the book and found two lines written, receipts for the mail that had been sent to his property. He took the book with him to the line to wait for the clerk. When summoned, he returned the smile for as long it was given him, before resuming his usual manner and they theirs. The clerk asked how she could help him. He asked what purpose the book served. She said his plan provided him with inferior benefits for a premium. He had just been lucky enough to see some of the measures they took to ensure he got the service he requested.

The book was set up after he had written his first piece of mail, and was consulted when dealing with any of his future deliveries. The troglodyte asked what other measures were taken, and was told it wouldn't be inferior service if she disclosed that information. The troglodyte told her there was a hack driver who used their lot. Hoping to tarnish the standing of the people that frequented the post office, bridge the gap between premium and inferior customers. The clerk didn't budge, divulged no other trade secrets to the troglodyte, and asked if there was anything else she could help him with. The troglodyte couldn't think of anything. She offered to dispose of the plastic he was carrying around, the post office had a direct route to the recycling facility. He said that the plastic had helped him out more than she had that day, then did his best not to hear her remark and he hurried out.

Having been made to feel inferior, the troglodyte took the plastic off his body and walked in the direction of his house. He kept his head down and was not disturbed by any people he passed, who thought he was suffering on account of his art project being destroyed. When he got to the property he put the vest near the goggles. He wondered if the people would have better understood him had he been wearing both. He went back outside and did his best to find the letter he had sent himself. When he wasn't able to find it, and considered the degradation a success, he cursed the post office for their little black book. He went to get his other piece of mail. He put the invitation back into the mail chute and let it slide to the middle.

Now when the postal worker came with the mail, barring any circumstance where they should successfully get it to the other side on their first try, will see the invitation while working to deliver the new mail, and will tell their superiors. The higher ups will then have to make a change to the book. In doing so they may wish to go back over the first transaction, to which the troglodyte would be ready. The post office would be able to provide documented proof that the troglodyte had indeed written and sent the letter, but he would be able to discover how their organization was set up from there on. How often the mail's whereabouts were accounted for after leaving the post office, and what protections were in place for the mail once it got to its destination. The troglodyte would say he never received the letter, and make every studious point possible to get the entry expunged.

The troglodyte took his bike to the train station and took the chain off before going inside. He wore the chain around his neck so it wouldn't be confused for a weapon, and if he had to be subdued would give his opponent the advantage. He headed straight for the food court and found a table without one of the fast food chain's logos to sit at. He didn't pledge any loyalties. His options weren't limited. The first food the troglodyte ordered from a burger chain, and he asked for a soda in his order. He took what he could carry back to his table. When he finished, he waited in line for two of the other chains and combined all of his plates before starting to eat.

When the troglodyte went back up to wait for a dessert, a shop in between the cluster he had already ordered from, he felt he was moving backwards. He was making no progress in line and began to fear he would miss dessert very soon, and the treat he was expecting would just become a snack. The troglodyte asked the person in front of him about the wait. They said they didn't know but would ask around. The question moved down the line until it was posed to the cashier, who gave the answer with the order, one of which sort of made it back to the troglodyte.

What the troglodyte was supposed to hear was that the machine was broken, but instead heard he must see it's motion. Since he had asked about the wait, the troglodyte took the answer to mean that the stuff made to order was good enough to justify the line, and that when they finally did move it only added to the experience, showing just how much effort and care each dessert required.

The person behind the troglodyte, who had noticed all the people in front of him speaking in secrecy, turned to the person behind them, and asked to find out how long the last link of the line had been waiting. The question made its way to the newcomer, who answered they had just got there. What was finally heard was, I absconder, so the person behind the troglodyte considered it a failed question and didn't expect to see the respondent at the end of the line. They could have been in waiting for years. The troglodyte turned around when was asked a question, the man having given up on concerning himself with the less fortunate behind him, and wanted to know what the troglodyte was going to order. The troglodyte said he was ready to give up, and didn't think he would hand the dessert chain any business. The man asked if he could have the troglodyte's spot then, and the line was set in motion

②0

The troglodyte went to the ticket window and asked the clerk about the other food courts at the different stations. The clerk said she could help the troglodyte with a train ticket but nothing more. The troglodyte bought a ticket for a later date, and asked the clerk to mail it to him when the date was approaching. She said she'd do her best to make sure it got to him. The safer option would be to get it today. The troglodyte gave a story about how he had lost a ticket that he was gifted many years ago, and so hadn't been able to reunite with an estranged relative. The clerk asked if they ever did reconnect, and the troglodyte passed on all the misfortune that his relative suffered after they weren't hosted. Which the troglodyte found out about through a letter. The troglodyte said that whenever he needs tickets he prefers to get them by mail because it gives them an air of importance.

The troglodyte left the ticket window showered with blessings from the clerk, who felt sorry for him and the pain he must be dealing with. She was taking his side by putting the blame on him as he had himself, and that if he hadn't lost the ticket maybe his relative's fate would have been different. The clerk's intentions would have come from the same place had the troglodyte performed a selfless deed, but may have had proud overtones rather than pity. The troglodyte checked the line for dessert before walking out of the station, noticing from the new angle that the people behind the counter were struggling to get their appliances to work.

The troglodyte walked the streets of the town without direction, and stopped when he saw the barkeep and the troupe of performers. They were on a front lawn stretching and doing light calisthenics. When the troglodyte approached them and was recognized, he was invited to see what they

had been working on. The barkeep told the troglodyte to clap
his hands steadily and with rhythm, and he was free to
choose how he did so. The troglodyte started clapping and
tried out different beats, until he was able to do one
consistently and confidently. When the barkeep and
performers heard that the troglodyte had found their rhythm,
they all began to dance around. It didn't look very
coordinated to the troglodyte. When they finished and asked
if the troglodyte liked the performance, he said he thought he
could do it better. The performer who had stuck up for him at
the bar previously, said that the troglodyte was actually the
performance, and that his response was the one they were
trying to elicit from all their viewers. By the observer
focusing on their own task and doing that well, they will
discover a feeling of authority when watching the performers
move by their hand.

The troglodyte asked if they could show him another act.
They accepted. With this one, nothing was to be required of
the troglodyte, except that he keep a safe distance away from
the demonstration once it began. The barkeep knelt in the
middle of the space, with his fingers interlocked. Another
performer stood next to him, his fingers interlocked and
positioned about a foot higher than the barkeep's. Two of the
other performers stood next to the barkeep and their
colleague, not using their hands for anything. With those
performers in position, the last one ran up to the barkeep, and
placing one hand in between his hands, began to do a
cartwheel down the line of performers. One hand first hit the
barkeep's, the other the person next to him, and then she
used the shoulders of the two remaining performers for her
feet, so the movement could continue. The barkeep and other
fingerlocker joined the rest, running down the line to offer

their shoulders for support as she was cartwheeled. For the finale, they formed a small circle and she dismounted in the middle. The troglodyte enjoyed this performance more than the first and was glad he saw it second.

After the troglodyte had finished watching the performers he continued walking, clapping his hands as he did so, experimenting with different rhythms. Some people he passed did a dance when they heard the troglodyte clapping. They looked like they were trying to get their feet to land right in their shoes. Some babies and infants mirrored his clapping when they came across him. Some teens began mock clapping at the troglodyte. Until each starting taking it seriously, thinking they had the better rhythm than their friends, and began to battle clap among themselves. The troglodyte stopped clapping when he heard a guitar close by and went to find where the sound emanated from. He walked until he was sure the source was just beyond the bushes impairing his view. Parting them with his hands, he saw the guitarist.

The woman playing looked to be just out of college. The troglodyte wondered how she must feel. He listened to her song, which reconciled past angst with a bright outlook from higher ground. Conditioned to think the future was too far off or much too soon, the girl was at a good time in her life for songwriting, and received applause from the troglodyte when she was done singing. She humbly hung her head and asked if the troglodyte played.

The troglodyte confessed he did not. He offered he never had the discipline to try. The girl nodded approvingly, and said that him realizing that proved he could still learn. The troglodyte explained he had no intentions to find the discipline required. Almost convincingly he said, the greatest discipline was to just be, having knowledge that self control only becomes available as needed, and the process could not be quickened. The girl asked if the troglodyte was talking about free will, to which he could provide no right or wrong answer, so didn't give one.

The girl began playing again when she saw the troglodyte trying to find an answer, and didn't interrupt his thoughts with her voice. The troglodyte listened, waiting for her to start with the lyrics while she waited for him to provide some inspiration. The stand off lasted for a few chord progressions until the troglodyte got up and started to leave. The girl stopped playing when she saw him attempting to find his way back out from the bushes, and said she could play something else. She knew plenty of songs. She asked if he was leaving because of her. The troglodyte turned, felt compelled to smile, and returned to a more open part of the park.

He saw a few kites flying in the sky, and deduced their owners were part of a group and not separate entities. One kite had a picture of a caterpillar, another with wings which resembled a butterfly, and the third a picturesque bowl of cereal. He figured the kite with cereal must be for the parent, and was their way of promoting a healthy diet. He wondered if the children ever swapped with each other, or if they always had to fly the same kite. He thought always flying the same kite would be difficult for their young egos. The caterpillar and butterfly's shortcomings would begin to show themselves if their backbone was contemplated for too long, and the children would surely become jealous of one another. In preparation for any aggravation, the parent had chosen to fly a bowl of cereal, so that the kids would know it could always be worse. The troglodyte stopped watching when the cereal kite and butterfly got tangled together, and were no longer able to fly. The parent may have been just as demonstrative during every outing, and was attempting to show the caterpillar was the one to be envied, for they could consume as much as they wished. They did their best to quiet the screaming child, who wanted to fly like a butterfly, and promised they would reward them if they would stop making a scene.

The troglodyte turned his attention to a water fountain and made his way towards it. He walked slowly, eyes never wavering from the water works, and his concentration was only broken when he needed to be conscious of the people around. Since it was the first time the troglodyte had seen the fountain, he tried to make it as memorable as possible and form an imprint. When he got to the fountain he sat with his back to it, feeling the mist on the back of his head and neck. There were a few other people sitting in the same manner as the troglodyte and he nodded to each of them. This in turn got them to all nod at each other, presumably for at least the second time.

He asked the person next to him why they chose to sit at the fountain. The person said it was their way of getting away from their significant other during their daily park routine. They were able to remain out of sight because of the fountain. When they reunite with their partner and asked where they had been hiding, they were able to truthfully answer that they hadn't been hiding at all and had been by the fountain all day. They were good with angles. They explained there were two other fountains in the park and they had yet to be discovered while away from their partner. The troglodyte asked what they would do once their partner developed a better system than they, relying less on guessing and more on a process of elimination to find them. The person answered that they would have to adapt their own system as well, and may have to move on foot to counter manoeuvre against their search party. One of the other people sitting near the troglodyte took his place in the conversation and soon everyone sitting at the fountain beside the troglodyte was discussing strategy.

For the rest of the time the troglodyte was in the park, he searched for the searchers, but did not interrupt them in their habitat. He didn't follow one for too long before tracking down another, not wanting to make his presence known. He guessed at which searcher was with which not to be rescued, but didn't wait to find out if he was correct in any of his assumptions. He left the park, after watching one of the searchers walking around a group of trees, their neck strained as much as their patience. It wasn't until later that night the troglodyte realized he had left his bicycle at the train station. He had to take the chain off of his neck before getting ready for bed.

He took out some money and headed for the roadway. He walked alongside his thumb, looking for a ride, and found transport in a vending truck with a beer logo on the back. The driver was a young man with a beard too long for his age. The food court was one of his stops. The troglodyte waited at two of the stops while the driver unloaded his truck. The driver didn't wait for the troglodyte when they made it to the train station, and drove off to another delivery. The troglodyte collected his spare parts and assembled his bike once back outside, in a vacant spot where beer used to be. He didn't blame the driver for leaving him, he had already stopped twice for a hitchhiker and anymore would have made the troglodyte something else. The troglodyte knew the driver was also on the clock and he hadn't thought to offer him a tip, which would have made the driver something else had he accepted. The troglodyte struggled getting his bike home, but the journey back to his house was made easier by having the bike. When he got back to his house he backed up the bike to the wall, moved his body over the handlebars and used the momentum to get the bike's back tire in the air, so he could walk the bike up the wall. He made sure the bike would stay put, before going to bed and falling asleep.

The troglodyte slept in the next morning, which saved the construction workers the hassle of having to deal with him. When the troglodyte did wake and wandered outside, he asked the workers who was in charge, followed their guidance, and asked the foreman how long the project would take. The foreman told the troglodyte it would take as long as it took, and the troglodyte asked if he could make it go faster. The foreman said they could do the job faster, but if it didn't take as long as it took then it may be left unfinished. The troglodyte said if it was left unfinished then it would take longer than it takes, and their working faster would give them the rest they so desperately needed, so that they could come back and finish the job. The foreman asked for the troglodyte's name, which the troglodyte didn't give him, shaking his head once to the side and not breaking eye contact. The foreman wondered what kind of man didn't offer up his name when asked. The troglodyte gave him some idea when he said a name is something that has been named, and since you cant name yourself, the troglodyte couldn't tell him his name.

The foreman asked why the troglodyte was in such a rush for the toll booths to be up. The troglodyte told him for the sake of the foreman's workers, who, if they weren't careful, would get boxed in, and have to pay the attendant who would arrive on time. The foreman excused himself from the troglodyte after explaining that his workers, being the ones that set up the machinery, could disable it once nearly finished, cross the border, then reengage.

The troglodyte went back to his house, grabbed a collapsible chair and sat in his backyard. He was angry that the foreman would, if necessary, delay finishing the project to get out of paying the toll. He kicked at an ant walking underneath his feet. He missed the ant but followed its path towards the hill it called home. He felt guilty for trying to kick at the ant, which could be so easily replaced, and took out his frustration on the chair he was sitting in. He threw the chair across the yard, followed it, and began to kick dirt up onto it. When his right leg started to tire he used his left, and only stopped once he was tired throughout. He then picked up the chair, turned it over, and collapsed it to bring to storage. He took one of his trash bags from it's box, struggled to open it because it had been sealed twice, and put the slightly damaged chair inside. He dumped the rest of the camping equipment, and anything he could safely remove from the obstruction, inside the bag as well. He then put the trash bag where the camping stuff used to be, and went to go sit on the steps in front of his house.

Some of the construction workers, who thought they knew a good tantrum when they saw one, waited to see if the troglodyte would do anything more. The troglodyte did nothing but sit on the steps. When he could no longer consider any progress to be made on the toll booth, because he had watched the process for too long, the troglodyte took the second path to town. He went to the farmer's house and was answered at the door by his daughter. The daughter said the farmer and her mother weren't home, and wanted to know where the troglodyte's head was.

He said he had come to check on the progress of their toll booth, and wanted permission to wander around the farmer's property. The girl said she knew no reasons to not allow the troglodyte to proceed, but asked that he didn't disturb any of the animals on his way to the outpost. The troglodyte asked if the animals were easily disturbed. The girl replied they were sensitive to disturbance but not easily frightened. The troglodyte asked what would happen if they did frighten. The girl said they would probably stampede, though any knowledge she had was second hand. The troglodyte took her warning seriously when he crossed the paths of the livestock. Stampedes were pure chaos. One involving animals who were not used to the practice could prove even more dangerous. And whereas in the wild more animals would join the collective as it passed, on the farm there were limited animals, so the ones stampeding would have to take on multiple roles.

When the troglodyte was clear of any goat, chicken or cow, he could see the toll booth being built. He casually walked up to it and leaned his body against it to rest. One of the workers asked him if he was trying to slow them down. If so, could he please refrain from doing so, they had a deadline to meet. The troglodyte said he liked the cut of their jib, and told him he wouldn't be a bother. He himself was only resting for a moment, while rushing in between deadlines. The man said there's no work like hard work and hard work likes no one. The troglodyte left the toll booth and walked the road that passed near his house, choosing fight over flight when concerned drivers honked at him. So as to not give in to the chaos.

The troglodyte saw a dead porcupine on his walk. He waited for the rush of traffic to subside, then dragged the carcass from the middle of the street to the gutter. The troglodyte dissected the animal, then moved his hands so he could have a look proper. It appeared the porcupine had been injured before stumbling out into the street, trying to flee their nemesis. The troglodyte closed the eyelids of the animal, whose eyes still shone a look of abject terror, then wondered if the spirit might prefer them open. He thought of it as like an actor on stage, who when the lights are on and the curtains drawn can't see the audience. But also is unable to see them when the lights are off and the curtains are closed. He opened the eye lids again, which wasn't as smooth a transition as when he closed them. He stepped back to see how he should leave it.

Now the eyes that looked back at him were questioning, as though they waited for the troglodyte to make the decision on how they should rest. He decided on closing them. So that they wouldn't shine like cloudy pearls of an oyster to any predator flying by, and began working on taking out the quills. Since the porcupine's body was no longer functioning as a cohesive unit, the troglodyte was easily able to pluck. Each pluck was accompanied by the sound of a popping cluck. He carried the bundle of quills back to his property without incident. The troglodyte went around the perimeter of his property, putting a quill in the ground every few steps, doing his best to remember the property line as it was. When he passed by the toll booth, he received strange looks but wasn't questioned by any of the workers. Once he had circled the property and found he still had quills left over, he started another lap, making it about halfway before his quiver was empty.

He didn't want to leave the job unfinished, but also didn't want to not finish the job. He headed for town, hoping to find something that could serve the same function as the porcupine quills. He went to a hardware store where he purchased hundreds of feet of very thin rope, some small reflector posts, and a bunch of reflectors. When he went to the cashier, he was told by someone who said they shouldn't be telling him, that all the material he was purchasing today could be found at any landfill or dump. The cashier told the troglodyte that he would be paying too much for what simple items he required. They couldn't sell it to him in good conscience. The troglodyte asked the cashier how they'd be able to live with themself, knowing they were taking food out of the owner's family's mouths by declining him the sale. The cashier told the troglodyte to take the stuff he needed and go. The cashier opened their wallet and deposited into the register. As the troglodyte walked back to his house he wondered if he had just taken food out of the mouth of the cashier, by allowing the owner of the hardware store to sit down with their family for a meal. He supposed it was the way it had to be, otherwise there would be such a thing as a free lunch.

The troglodyte put the posts with reflectors down where he had left off putting the quills, and finished securing his property. He took the reflectors and put them onto every quill, then weaved the rope between the quills and reflector posts. The quills weren't strong enough to support the rope off the ground, so it snaked the property. The troglodyte walked around the property to observe the reflections and the way they all played off of each other. He then took his focus off the reflectors and sauntered around, looking at anything but. He was double checking his periphery. When he was standing by the road and walking, he could see the reflectors in the corner of his eye. He thought that might help to keep the drivers safe and honest. They could be casually driving along, even with eyes on the road, and think something is approaching from their right. Bombarded with adrenaline in however many seconds it takes before they look to see what caused the release. When they bring into focus not another vehicle but just a reflector, they will resume driving with greater vigor and clarity. Of course, as with the troglodyte's previous plans concerning the road, this one could backfire. The driver may jerk the wheel when the reflector is seen, instead of their head, and could cause an accident. The troglodyte didn't let his mind go down that path, just as he hadn't questioned why the porcupine crossed the road.

②1

The troglodyte had a light meal for supper that night and read his book while he ate. He read over the blue notes since he had been transcribing the red. When he found them to be of similar style and content, he realized the colors weren't profound. They didn't signify anything and were inconsequential. So he started to copy the blue notes from the beginning, after the red notes on the page, until he realized if he thought like that he would end up with the whole book copied word for word. Once his blue notes had caught up with the red. He turned to the back of the book and began copying his notes by working his way up the page. This way he would be able to read the effects first and then uncover the causes, turning his notes into a mystery. He went to bed after copying, the wind whistles catcalls, while the ocean dances for moon.

He woke in the middle of the night and got out of bed to have a drink of water. The full moon allowed him to see the reflectors glowing red around his property. It looked to the troglodyte as if hundreds of abnormally large eyes were staring back at him. He held the image at the front of his mind while he drifted off. When the troglodyte awoke in the morning the construction crew was already nearby and looked to be close to finished with the toll booth. The troglodyte noticed that none of the trucks had parked inside of the toll line. He was relieved.

He didn't mind the workers not paying the toll if they were on foot, since their weight was far less than a vehicle's and wouldn't ask as much of the road. The troglodyte did see one car pull up and park on the inside, and judging from the reflective vest exiting the car, knew the woman to be the attendant. The troglodyte ran into his house to collect the

coin carrier he had made. He hurried to the toll booth once
he saw the attendant had made her way inside. The
troglodyte tapped on the window of the toll booth, held the
coin carrier next to the glass and raised his eyebrows as if to
say he was leaving something unsaid. The attendant tried to
shoo him away, but the troglodyte was persistent and his
glass tapping finger strong, so she slid open the window to
assure him the toll booth wasn't open yet. He would have
more time to find coins to for his passage. The troglodyte
explained that the coin carrier was actually a gift for her. It'd
be she who'd have time to collect coins. She saw how
determined the troglodyte was to give her the purse. She
accepted it, scolding him that he shouldn't have. The
troglodyte responded that it was nothing.

He asked her how long she had been letting pass and
taking names. She confided it was her first time as an
attendant. She had previously been an understudy to a
successful actress, whose advice to her was to study as many
faces as possible. The attendant had tried other jobs where
she had had to interact with many different people, but was
hoping that the toll booth gig would prove to be the key to
the actors guild kingdom.

The troglodyte left the toll booth once the attendant had
settled in. He saw her put the coin carrier within arms reach
on a desk. She said she was only working a half day but was
required to watch the introductory training video that had
been provided her. Although the troglodyte was curious to
see what on the job training would be like, he said goodbye
and went into town. Headed for the office. It began to rain.
He without umbrella, his clothes got soaked through, causing
him to apologize to each person he passed while in the office.
The noise his wet clothes made when he walked disturbed

the people of the office, who upon hearing him broke off from their conversations. They quickly accepted the troglodyte's apologies, said they'd allow it, and watched him slosh on. When the troglodyte reached the secretary she beat him to an apology, saying she felt sorry the troglodyte was so unprepared for any weather.

She nodded to the umbrella she had nearby and said she never left her place without it. The troglodyte said her priorities were wrong. She should never be leaving the office without it. She didn't laugh when she said she never left the office without her keys, and that some days even doing that was a struggle. The troglodyte left the secretary and said things were already starting to turn around. His clothes were a little more discreet after drip drying. He really noticed the effect while waiting in line for the council. Water that should have been able to drip freely was being contained in the folds of his clothes during movement. So as the line moved forward, the troglodyte did his best to forward march while staying as vertical as possible.

The troglodyte listened to each step he took, and adjusted his gait accordingly to the sounds his clothes made. If the sound was noticeable to people other than himself, he knew he was moving too fast and wasn't giving the droplets a chance to break free. With his increased focus on auditory perception, the troglodyte heard someone excusing themself to the people waiting in line. They were announcing they had a friend who was saving them a spot. As the voice grew nearer, the troglodyte knew he must be the referred to friend and braced for what was to come.

The friend of a friend stopped beside the troglodyte. When the troglodyte slowly revolved his head around to look at the chameleon, it said that people have legs so they don't have to swim. It looked around the line hoping for a laugh, but received none from the people still angry with it for pushing them back. The troglodyte let out a dry cough to let it know he would've laughed if he could, and said it must have him confused with someone else. The chameleon said it didn't think so, and began telling the troglodyte the story of why it had to see the council. After hearing the tale, the troglodyte said he still thought the chameleon had him confused. He was put on the defensive when the chameleon raised it's voice, and pleaded for the troglodyte to remember it. The troglodyte knew he didn't know any chameleons, though he knew they knew how to argue for the sake of arguing. Their argument lasted a couple minutes. The troglodyte ended up leaving the line. The chameleon got the spot it was looking for. Justice for the people waiting to be served.

When the troglodyte passed the secretary, she asked what the commotion had been. She asked if it had caused his quick departure. The troglodyte said there was a quarrel between lost friends and he hadn't the heart to stick around to bear witness. The secretary asked the troglodyte if he wanted to talk more about it. He declined, left the floor, and took the stairs up to the roof.

It was still raining when the troglodyte got to the roof, though not nearly as hard as before. He stood near the edge, looked down at the street below, brought both his hands together as hard as he could and yelled Shango. A child looked up at the troglodyte when they heard the exclamation, and asked their parent what the troglodyte was doing. The parent grabbed the child's hand and pulled them away hurriedly, telling them working in an office was difficult on rainy or sunny days. The troglodyte must have felt he deserved a break. After the troglodyte had yelled from the rooftop, he went back down the stairs without entering any of the floors, and sat on the steps in front of the office building. He felt guilty for sitting under an overhang during a storm, so left the steps to head for the furniture store. He had never been to the camping store, so asked the staff of the store he was at for directions. The person that helped him was friendly. They invited the troglodyte to wait for the storm to subside in the store. The troglodyte said he would like to, but feared his legs would begin to cramp if he was made to stand in one place. He feared the absence of walking, and said to avoid it he would be on his way.

The staff offered him a mechanic's jumpsuit if he would change out of his clothes and peruse their inventory. The troglodyte accepted the offer and found a comfortable bed to lay on. A shopper walked by him as he was beginning to fall asleep. They looked around for the artist who had staged the scene. When the shopper couldn't find anyone nearby other than furniture store employees, who she didn't figure for artists, she asked one about the bed the troglodyte was in. She bought the model and was able to take a piece of art home with her. When the troglodyte woke up from the impromptu nap, he was told he had helped in one of their sales. They had decided to let him sleep because of it. They said that ordinarily if someone were to fall asleep in the store, they would either call the authorities, convinced the person was a derelict, or, attempt to guilt them into a sale if they appeared to be of well off means. The troglodyte asked to have the directions repeated before he left the store, in search of some wealthy uncle with a camping hobby.

He made it to the camping store without needing to ask for any more directions and found what he was looking for immediately upon entering. He grabbed three umbrellas, each a different brand and slightly different style, and headed for the check out line. When he was asked if he found everything okay, he said he found it even better than that. They had put together a nice outfit for themselves. They gave the troglodyte his change, which he swung around in his pocket exiting the store.

He opened one umbrella, and held the other two upside down against it's handle so he could still use his other hand. He walked back to the center of town and was approached by more than a few people, who thought he was making the noise with the change in his pocket for their benefit. To draw attention and solicit a sale. The troglodyte didn't stop his pocket music after turning down each request for a sale, which invited other arrogants to try their own hands. Although the troglodyte didn't sell any of his umbrellas, he did trade one with a teen that he passed. The teen goosed him into the trade by saying, that since they were still growing and the troglodyte was not, it made sense for the troglodyte to trade down in size. The troglodyte told the teen they were too big for their own shoes. He accepted the trade and closed the umbrella as he handed it off.

The teen opened the closed umbrella handed them and left as soon as it was in their grasp. When the troglodyte reached the center of town, he watched people spinning their umbrellas. Any persons behind a spinner would get soaked unless they positioned their own umbrella defensively. When the victims found an opening, they in turn spun their own umbrella, rather than confront their victimizer. It was easier to be both victim and victimizer than one or the other. The troglodyte kept his eyes peeled for the reaction and made sure to keep a safe distance when walking behind a potential defective mud flap. Seeing all the spinning umbrellas and wet hair got the troglodyte thinking about the barber shop. He headed that way. When he got to the barbershop he stood outside and watched the rotating sign for some rotations. He was sad to see the white had been marked up, but understood that the curious were apt to use the scientific method.

The troglodyte sat down in a barber's chair and asked if a little could be taken off the top. The barber reached for his wallet, but then said sure, and began to grab his clippers. He stopped when the troglodyte started ranting, gesticulating his head animatedly. The troglodyte was going on about how the barbershop missed out on potential business. He had almost missed an idea, and said he would have, if not for one of his walks on a street. The troglodyte wanted the barbershop to produce a handful of more rotating signs with a few slight alterations.

The rotating signs design spinning around his head, was for two strands of mirror to replace the red and white pattern. Because of the strange angles of the mirrors, anyone who happened across them would see a distorted view of themself. Upon looking in the mirror and the self reflection it entails, they will be shown hope by the reminder the sign provides. There are barbershops, and there is one right around the corner. When they walk to the barbershop, the image they saw in the mirror will be fresh in their minds. Seeing the old fashioned red and white they will be overcome with relief. The chances of them deciding not to get a haircut at that point would be very slim.

The troglodyte said that for his plan to be maximally effective, the signs would have to be placed on the surrounding buildings. Out of view of the barbershop but not too far off. Each mirror would be an equal distance apart, so not to discourage the potential customer each time they saw a new mirror, but actually strengthen their resolve to find the barbershop. When the troglodyte finished talking, the barbershop was completely quiet. The troglodyte broke first and asked the barber what he thought of the idea. The barber said he would have to think about it, but in the meantime, wanted to know what the troglodyte wanted to have done to his hair.

The troglodyte told the barber to take all the time he needs, but warned him that if he sat on his hands for too long he'd forget he had any. The troglodyte asked for a shave. Only when he had left the chair was his idea discussed. One of the customers told the barber there was no precedent for what the troglodyte had proposed, and the barber would have to be crazy to give it any further consideration. The customer was lucky they were a regular or the barber may have nicked them on accident, surprised by their audacity and reacting unconsciously.

...

The troglodyte went from the barbershop to the department of public works and closed his umbrella very calmly outside the doors, smiling at the clerk and showing his humility. When the troglodyte went up to the desk, he said he was interested in sitting in on a safety class. Where it was shown how safety when run its course can help you to lead a better life. The clerk told him to take a form to identify his reason for visit, and that once completed she could have him an answer. The troglodyte took the form and allowed the woman to make a phone call. He pretended to fill out the form so as to not be rude to the clerk, who didn't want to be rude to him, and had given him the form to keep him occupied while she had had to excuse herself. When the troglodyte saw the clerk hang up the phone he approached the desk and asked if the call was about him. She asked who was asking and offered her hand to him so that he may release the form.

He said he was a concerned citizen, who feared that his path in life may lead him to be prone to accidents. He would like to live responsibly. The clerk checked the form and asked the troglodyte why he hadn't written any of that down. He said the pen was mightier than the sword, and that that was valuable information in her profession. The clerk said that since there were only three six hour classes, that she couldn't permit him to sit in on one. If there had been six three hour classes, she may have tried to make an exception. He would need to pay an enrollment fee and fill out the form, was the best she could do. The troglodyte asked if he could do some type of work for them to cover the fee, with a caveat that it could not in the least way be unsafe. The caveat to his caveat was his broad categorization, including office type accidents like an exploding pen. The clerk thought the conditions were too difficult to meet. She said the ballpoint pen is even mightier because it can be refilled. The sword must always be sharpened, regardless of which type of pen.

The troglodyte left the department, opening his umbrella before he was even through the doorway. The troglodyte kept a safe distance away from the umbrella wielders on the street and made his way towards the river. The troglodyte looked for rocks he could skip, poking at the ground with one of his spare umbrellas. He had the other two, one in use, in his other hand. When he had fifteen or so stones, he opened his prodding umbrella violently to clear it of any debris, before turning it upside down. He left it open so he would have a dry place to sit.

He skipped one stone. He immediately knew he had spent more time finding it then watching it skip, and did his best to make better with the next one. The stones he skipped in the middle were closest in time to how long it had took to uncover them, having found them all within the same area, while the last stones he skipped were much like the first. The troglodyte was positioned so that the normal sized umbrella shielded him, while the small one carried no water because of it's size. The third one was on the ground next to him until the troglodyte had finished skipping the stones, and could make use of both his hands again.

The troglodyte watched rain hit the river water, and realized if he had done that first he may have never searched for the rocks. Watching the rain didn't inspire him to gather more stones and he stood up so he could close the small umbrella. The troglodyte followed the river to the bait and tackle garage. The owner yelled to him and made a quip about the weather. When the troglodyte was inside the garage, the owner eyed the umbrellas and immediately knew where the troglodyte had got them.

The owner asked if the troglodyte had used the discount that his family had. The troglodyte responded that he thought the seller's family had a bad stroke of luck and hadn't inherited any secrets. The owner said it wouldn't be half bad to not inherit any secrets, then realized that the troglodyte wasn't talking as figuratively as the owner was thinking, and was referring to the water plant. The owner said he thought the troglodyte knew his family had the discount for the camping store. He asked if he hadn't made that clear on the previous visits. The owner excused the troglodyte's absentmindedness, and said that he could buy back the umbrellas from him. At a higher price than he had had to pay even. The troglodyte agreed to sell him the smaller one and the spare, and said he wanted a cooler to be ready for him next time he fished. The owner said he could use any cooler on display or those considered stock, but couldn't promise there would be ice, or that the cooler's lid wouldn't have been open all day. The troglodyte asked if there were any other discounted secrets that the seller could loose, and was told that mention of the seller's name and family still held weight around the town. The troglodyte asked whether to include the first name with the family name. The owner said that would have to be decided on a case by case basis. The troglodyte asked if he could take some fish stew for the road. The seller was delighted the troglodyte had asked without being offered. He made a mental note to heat up a bowl whenever he saw the troglodyte approaching the garage, just as a real estate agent might put cookies in an oven before a show.

The troglodyte walked back to his house with the dinnerware under his arm, and enjoyed his meal once out of the rain. He circled around the open floor when finished, before going to bed.

②2

The next morning the troglodyte woke, he took a case of water out to the attendant in the toll booth. The attendant was reading a newspaper in between her charges, and the troglodyte asked if there was anything interesting about what she read. The attendant said that in the capital city, a mobile zoo had been shut down and the city were trying to find a home for the animals now without one. The troglodyte asked if it said where the mobile zoo had been set up, and stated it must have been in the same location for a while. Since the sting had taken place. The attendant put down the newspaper as she gave a driver their change, and raised the gate.

When she resumed reading the newspaper and couldn't find where the mobile zoo had been located, she brought up another story to the troglodyte, who only half listened to what she was saying. When she stopped reading the article and waited for the troglodyte to find it interesting, he asked if she wouldn't mind giving a water bottle to the next customer that visited her window. She agreed to, but told the troglodyte to keep the case of water bottles outside the toll booth with him. If the customers refused the bottle he must remain calm.

The driver pulled up, and after paying the attendant, was surprised to hear the troglodyte call to them through the window behind the woman. The driver was confused when offered a water bottle and asked the attendant if the troglodyte was with her, and if the water was safe to drink. The attendant handed the driver the bottle, said there was nothing wrong with it other than it may be a bit warm, and told the driver to have a nice day. When the driver had continued on the toll road, the woman asked what the troglodyte hoped to gain by giving out free water through her window. The troglodyte explained that it just seemed right. When another driver pulled up, the exchange was repeated almost to the letter, but this time the driver noticed the troglodyte. What's worse is that they had seen him before, walking or pedaling on the toll road.

They asked the troglodyte why he dove out of the way when he heard car horns honk. The troglodyte said a child eats for their parent's benefit, without knowing they're doing it for themselves. When the driver had been at the toll booth window for longer than the people waiting in line thought they should, the waiters began to honk. The troglodyte hit the ground. He momentarily lost his breath when he landed on the case of water, which somewhat helped to soften his fall. The driver was satisfied and held up the line for no longer, checking their rear-view about a half dozen times as they drove off. The attendant took care of the customers that had been waiting, giving them slightly damaged water bottles handed to her through the window. When the attendant had a moment to herself, she asked the troglodyte if he planned on charging anyone for the product. He said that he was just conducting a trial run at the moment. He still needed to come up with a business plan for moving forward. The troglodyte asked if he could borrow the newspaper from the attendant, took it, and headed into town.

He reread the newspaper as he walked but never got past the first page, having found the address to where the newspaper was published on the very front. When he got to the hack station he asked them to take him to the publishing house. He skimmed the rest of the paper while along for the ride. The hack driver asked the troglodyte if there was anything interesting in it. The troglodyte told them that what was being discussed was interesting but not the way it was written about. He gave the example of the mobile zoo, and said the investigator had not answered any of the questions the troglodyte had had about how the operation was run.

The hack driver said that the paper was not meant to inform, necessarily, but instead guide the reader into asking questions about what they were reading. If the subscriber writes to the paper and asks questions about a previous issue, the staff at the paper will be able to better cover their next story. Extraordinarily market their next piece. The driver said they themself could have provided proof that this was their practice. Unfortunately they no longer had the letter they had sent the journals, which would have shown all that all they had taken issue with was covered in the next edition.

The troglodyte thought of his post office book, but didn't mention it to the driver. He didn't want to offend them by offering inferior insights for a premium. The troglodyte exited the hack when it arrived at the publishing house, and told the driver he could keep whatever was left in the case of water. The troglodyte said that if the driver let the case sit in the backseat of his car for long enough, then give their customers the bottles, they may be able to write into the newspaper and give them an inside scoop for their next story. The troglodyte took the newspaper with him, tucked under his arm as he entered the building.

He was surprised that more people in the office weren't carrying newspapers themselves. Then he noticed there were newspapers all around him, and it was probably just as easy to pick one up and find your place. He put his own copy down, at the desk of a busied worker jamming fingers on the keyboard. He asked where he could find the billing department. The employee said that everyone who worked in the building had to wear multiple hats, and she should be able to help him. Her terminal was as suited for the job as anyone's.

The troglodyte said that he hadn't been receiving the newspaper lately, and thought that his subscription had been canceled, until he found today's news right on his doorstep. The woman looked at the name on the back of the newspaper, then entered the information into the system. She told the troglodyte that there was still a subscription and asked if the address that she had was the correct one. The troglodyte told her that it was not and that that explained the absence, and gave her the information for his updated address. The employee handed the troglodyte back his newspaper and asked if there was anything else she could do for him. He asked about the mobile zoo. She said that since it was an ongoing investigation she wasn't able to divulge anything new. Public relations was not one of her hats. What was in the paper had already been cleared by the authorities, but the paper hadn't been able to produce any more evidence. The troglodyte thanked her for helping him and asked if he might be able to see where the newspapers are printed. She told him that that part of the building was closed to the public, but there was plenty of reading material available to him about the process. The troglodyte took a handful of brochures with him as he left the office.

The troglodyte walked around outside of the publishing house and tried to find a story. He approached people that were going about their day and stated that he was with the newspaper, handing them a brochure as he made his claim. He asked them if they had any news they would like to share. For he was starting a new editorial section. The pieces would feature people who read the news but never considered themself to be newsworthy. The troglodyte would show them in the best possible light to make them so. If the troglodyte were to really write these editorials he would have had a hard time ahead of him. The responses he got were as expected, and yearned to be something more.

Someone relayed to the troglodyte his own story, but with the details very wrong. So the troglodyte didn't realize they had been talking about him until much later, after he had left their company. The troglodyte was ultimately glad that he was not a reporter and thought the job would be a difficult one. The people reading the newspaper would almost certainly not want to hear stories about themselves, having not found their life very interesting or noteworthy, but want to read about a higher subset of people. They are imaginative as can be regarding celebrities, and put them in a league of their own. They are really reading about themselves dressed up. It is the job of the reporter to turn the ordinary into extraordinary, and disguise their actual talent pool. The troglodyte was nearly rid of all the brochures, then one of the higher ups of the newspaper asked him to leave the property. They tried to convey to the people with company brochures in hands, that the troglodyte was not a representative of the newspaper and was in no way affiliated. The troglodyte gave the higher up the rest of the brochures and wondered what other roles they played in the company. Or if the higher ups were allowed to skate by with only one field of study.

②3

The troglodyte went to the deli and ordered a sandwich. He ate at the part of the deli counter that was separated for doing so, and listened to the plastic slices tear apart from one another by the butcher's hand. He gave the butcher a big tip when he was done eating and left the newspaper where he was sitting. When the butcher called after him telling him of his mistake, the troglodyte said there hadn't been one. The paper was left opened to the article on the mobile zoo.

The troglodyte's next stop was an animal shelter that was on the outside of the town. He was greeted by anxious barks when he approached the kennel. The troglodyte felt sorry he couldn't take an animal home with him. In the past he would have had no problem adopting a pet, when his life had been secluded and serene. He knew it would be irresponsible to adopt one now. The troglodyte asked to be shown those available anyway, and knelt down beside the cages offering treats that had been provided. The troglodyte asked the volunteer how many bags of treats are given out to prospective hand feeders each day. She said she didn't know but could find out for him. The troglodyte dismissed her offer and asked her which dog she liked best. She pointed to one who was obviously being overfed. The troglodyte guessed that was everyone's favorite. The troglodyte asked to see some of the more exotic animals at the shelter, but the woman said cats and dogs were all they had. The volunteer showed the troglodyte to the room with the cats, but he began to sneeze uncontrollably and felt a scratch in his throat. The troglodyte realized he must have a cat allergy, which made him wonder what exactly he had been going after with his traps set in the woods. He hadn't experienced any similar reactions while he was stalking his game, and figured that even if he approached the traps hours or days after they were uncovered, he still would have been sensitive to the allergens.

The troglodyte left the animal shelter receiving the same farewell as how he'd been greeted from the penned animals outside, and headed back to his property. He went back to the toll booth and returned the attendant her paper, saying he had changed the address so that the paper would be delivered to him instead of her. She asked why he did this, and he told the story of how the secretary didn't leave her house without an umbrella but wasn't as strict in her routine when leaving the office. If the paper was delivered to the troglodyte's house, then the attendant wouldn't have to worry about leaving her place without it, and could be sure to have it when it was needed. The attendant looked in the direction of the troglodyte's house. She asked where his mailbox was.

The troglodyte remembered the old practice of throwing newspapers onto lawns. He pointed to the ditch, curious of the woman's new line of questioning. She didn't see a mailbox and told the troglodyte the postal worker wouldn't be able to deliver without one. He explained that he and the post office had an understanding, and the less she knew about it the better. The attendant gave up on the subject, and told him that customers had been asking for water bottles since he had left. She told him that since her shift was almost over he needn't worry about going to get more, and that the troglodyte should stay around to meet her replacement. The troglodyte asked if she was going to leave the paper for the replacement, to which she said if he asked she would. The troglodyte went back into his house to get a case of water and left it with the attendant. He heeded her to fill in the replacement on their operation.

After the troglodyte left the tollbooth, he was surprised to find the couple waiting for him in his backyard. They were sitting on the ground, and got up when they saw the troglodyte, to tell him that they were in the neighborhood. The troglodyte took this to mean that they had either been at the farm or had taken their vehicle off-roading to get around paying the toll. He didn't see any car nearby so chose to assume the former, and asked if they had bought any fresh eggs or cuts of meat. They plainly told the troglodyte no, unsure of the reference, and explained that they had been hiking through the woods.

They hadn't seen any wildlife but had seen signs that they had been there, none of which were edible. The couple mentioned they were going to the reopening of the buffet, since they were on the subject of food, and asked the troglodyte if he wanted to go along with them. The troglodyte said he had already tried to go to the first one and would only arrive late to this one, if he went at all. The couple said the restaurant had been one of their favorites, before it temporarily closed down, and they wanted to be as close to the front of the line as possible. The troglodyte walked the couple around to the front of the house when they were ready to leave. He told them he may see them there, although they may not see him, because he would inevitably be at one of the worst tables, while they at the best. The couple said if that was to be the case then the troglodyte should join them, to which the troglodyte said nothing, but tried to display his comprehension through body language.

When each of the three had said their, wells, and let the silence grow from there, the couple walked back into the woods and headed for the restaurant. The troglodyte went to the mail chute to check if the original invitation for the reopening was still there, and upon finding it, left it untouched. He knew the postal worker would have to come to deliver the paper, and if what the attendant said was true and it was delivered to the same place as the mail, the postal worker would surely notice the invitation. He practiced a few rounds with the bellows, and pushed out any thoughts that the postal worker wasn't getting paid enough. Nor could they ask for a raise, because the post office expected them to do the bare minimum for the inferior customers.

The troglodyte put his feet and hands into the mail slots, once his arms had sufficiently warmed up, and positioned his body horizontally. He moved sideways, rather than vertically as he had done before. While in the ditch, the troglodyte was hidden from view of passing cars on the toll road. He was as thankful for the privacy as he was able to be. He could do as he wished without others wishing to know what he did. When he climbed out of the ditch, he looked over at the toll booth and saw the same attendant from the day, now lit up in the box during the night. He walked over to the attendant for the third time that day and demanded to know where her replacement was. She said her superiors had called and asked if she was afraid of the dark. She said no. They said she could take tomorrow off.

The troglodyte asked did she mind having to change her plans. She winced, and said that only the worst plans are left unchanged. She updated the troglodyte on the water bottles sales, all sold, but hadn't asked for payment. Accepting cash donations instead. She had collected enough to cancel out the cost of buying the case. The troglodyte refused the money she offered. The troglodyte told her that the next time she worked she should offer the water bottles at full price, but let customers know their own bottle can be filled for free. The troglodyte would collect the bottles just used to fill the customer's own, now empty, and told the attendant she could keep whatever money she made. When the attendant said it may take too long to fill the customer's already empty bottles with their full ones, until they emptied, the troglodyte said he would work on expediting the process. For now they would have to make do. The troglodyte wished the attendant a good night and headed back into town. Bracing himself for any fiasco he may face over food.

4

The troglodyte stayed some distance away from the restaurant before he approached, weary of the two competing parties occupying the exterior. He saw the couple near the front of the line, just where they thought they wanted to be. The troglodyte knew that if tonight were anything like that previous night, being boxed in against the restaurant could be the worst spot for them. Luckily, the restaurant doors opened and ushered them inside, allowing the faces to change of the people waiting in line. Not those protesting. The troglodyte whisked over to the line once he saw the couple had made it inside, and was sure there wouldn't be trouble. The protesters were trying a new method to hammer home their old point, and had set a table up outside of the restaurant where three people sat. Another table was close by with plates on it.

One of the people sitting, would stand and go to the table with plates on it, while the two remaining sitters would both become occupied with themselves. One person mimed picking up a phone and talking animatedly. The other playacted drawing on a map, before eating the writing utensil. Once the actor had begun to swallow the imaginary marker, the food retriever would turn around, show a look of terror, and rush back to their pretend child. The distracted phone dialler will notice something isn't right and stow their phone. The three would then run off down the street, the child in the scene taking small quick steps, but all believably frantic. This scene was repeated over and over again. It may have hurt their cause more than it helped.

Any interest in the group running to the imaginary hospital was lost, because the actors would turn around once out of site of the restaurant, and walk back as if there was no emergency. Those that were interested, would follow the performers and ask questions. They never received any answers from the silent mimes, so would content themself to waiting in line at the restaurant. The people there could explain what the actors were trying to do. Even after hearing the controversy from restaurant goers, the newly arrived to the party decided to stay, wanting dinner after the show.

When the troglodyte was finally seated and properly tucked into a corner, he asked for water when the drink order came. He saw that the couple would likely not notice him from where they were sitting. He heaved a sigh of relief and looked some more around the restaurant. When the server came back with his water, he asked where the coloring utensils and place mats were. The server said that they were back ordered. The restaurant was hoping to have the new materials soon. They had been made aware of the scarcity of writing utensils able to bypass the digestion system, once they discovered the problem that quite a few other restaurants already had.

It took a long time for the food processing plant to agree with the office supply industry about the schematics for the new design. Once they announced they had reached an agreement, they had already sold out all pre-ordered. Now whenever a restaurant requests the new utensil they are put on a waiting list, to which the buffet establishment was now part of. The troglodyte asked if there were any other alternatives to keep him entertained. The server said she could have the cook burn his order if he would only place it. He could then spend his time working at cutting apart whatever it was to be, and attempt to chew it fine enough to be swallowed. The troglodyte said that would have to do, and asked that the chef make the most challenging thing on the menu. If he had asked for the easiest, there was a chance it wouldn't be forgot about and get burnt. The server left the troglodyte's table, took the orders of a few more, and returned to the kitchen.

The troglodyte got up from his table while he was waiting for something to kill time with, and headed for the buffet in search of any good leftovers. He didn't spend much time at the buffet line and returned to the security of the dark, where he could be mistaken for himself but not easily recognized. He surveyed the restaurant, and the people sitting which made it so, and tried to judge whether they were eating food from the buffet or made to order. Since he couldn't tell the difference, he was a little apprehensive about his meal to come, which would easily identify him as someone who had ordered. He guessed his plate would not acceptable for the sales floor. For this same reason, the troglodyte knew without a doubt whether the plates the server carried were for him, even though he wasn't sure what he ordered. He watched the server handle the tables that had ordered after him before bringing him his plate. She was too embarrassed to show it around the other customers.

The troglodyte worked furiously at cutting up his food. He would have stifled his grunts had he been able to help it. When his food was cut up into portions that with a normally textured food would have been much too small, he gave his jaw a workout trying to chew them. He wrapped his arm around his plate, huddling done while he ate, appearing to have something others covet. He watched people from the tables around him head back to the buffet line for seconds and thirds, while he worked on his first. The water that he hadn't yet touched was put to good use and allowed him the saliva to overcome his obstacle. The server passed by the

troglodyte a few times while he did something that
resembled eating, but thought it better not to disturb him, in
this his chosen form of entertainment.

When she saw that he had finished his plate, she
approached. He was told he was free to take anything he
wanted from the buffet, but he had to go now. The owners
had informed her they needed him to leave so they could sit
waiting customers. The troglodyte said he would pay their
tab if he was permitted to stay, but the woman said she
wasn't able to accommodate him. The troglodyte went to the
buffet line and spent as much time as he could looking over
the various food choices, hoping that the couple was still
there and would notice him. When he was not recognized or
asked to join anyone at their table, the troglodyte admitted
defeat and left the restaurant. He nodded to everyone he
passed that was waiting in line, then waited for the actors to
make their route to the hospital before pretending to chase
after them, wagging his fist.

When the actors turned around to head back to the
restaurant, the troglodyte continued on the street they were
taking. He preferred the atmosphere once back outside to
that of the better dining experience he had been denied at the
restaurant. The streetlamps were lit. The traffic lights looked
bold. He stopped by a couple of people who were outside
their apartment building having a smoke. He interrupted their
scheduled programming and asked why they were as they
were. In typical smoker fashion they pulled on their
cigarettes before answering. Blowing the smoke out of the
corner of their mouths. Preparing answers with some weird
look one can only find while focusing on their breath. The
look they wouldn't be able to give if they had been asked the

question without having their smoke. Their eyes were towards the ground in those seconds before an answer.

One of the smokers said that they were high strung and cigarettes took the edge off. The other said they did it for the opposite reason, and got adrenaline from cigarettes. They met somewhere in the middle after each having their smoke. The troglodyte thought their company must be unbearable if they were without. The troglodyte didn't ask for a cigarette and walked the streets until he found another person smoking and repeated his question. He didn't find their answer intriguing enough, and went to the motel where he hoped to find a more enticing sentiment.

The motel gave him a smoking room again, and he took a cigarette from the night manager. Though the reason they gave wasn't any better. He put the cigarette behind his ear and left it there. Sleeping on his other side when that time came. When he woke the next morning he tried noticing a difference in how he felt, having the cigarette so close to his airways all night. He left the motel and headed back to his house, unable to provide any remarkable answers when asked what the deal with the cigarette was.

When he got back to his property he saw the postal worker standing over the ditch. The postal worker was trying to get the newspaper to the other side of the mail chute, but wasn't able to find the right amount of force to do so. He went from smacking his hands together aggressively, to quick motions, to wiping off his brow. Having no luck working the bellows for the task. The troglodyte relieved him of the job, said that the newspaper was for him and he could take it off the worker's hands. The carrier agreed to the help, then informed the troglodyte there was still a piece of mail in the chute that had been delivered, but that the troglodyte hadn't received. The troglodyte glumly acknowledged the letter, before asking if the postal worker had to keep a special log for the troglodyte's deliveries.

The worker was taken aback by the accusation. He said he did as he was told and told not to say as he did. The carrier excused himself from the troglodyte, duty calls, and told him he'd appreciate it if he were there again to receive the newspaper next time. The troglodyte said he'd think about it. He took the newspaper to his front steps, where he sat and worked on the brain teasers in the back. He flew threw the wordsearch, made good time on the crossword, which was complete but not entirely accurate, and stared at the page with number puzzles. He read, read, and read again the directions, for they had no sway in his head, closed the paper and put it by his front door. So he wouldn't forget to give it to the attendant he knew. He walked across his property to the one he didn't know and introduced himself, before saying they must be the new means to an end.

The attendant asked the troglodyte where his car was, and after hearing his reply, said that he was a means to an end but not for the troglodyte. The troglodyte wanted to know if anyone had been asking about the water bottles, and if so maybe the attendant could actually help the troglodyte out. The attendant said they had, and he had been wondering the reason for it since his shift started. The troglodyte explained to him the details of his and the other attendant's plan, but was cut off when his listener wasn't interested. The attendant said that in the heat of the day people may be concerned about water. It was different at night. He didn't want to agree to be bothered nonstop, by people with whom his encounters were meant to be brief, and told the troglodyte he wouldn't be a part of it. The troglodyte implored that he at least sell and offer to refill the customers during his shift that day, since he had called out last night. The troglodyte muttered he wouldn't ask for anything else, and so was believed. The troglodyte went to fetch the a case of water without waiting for a response and slid it through the toll booth window when he returned.

    The troglodyte used his workbench to make what was perhaps his easiest reprurposed plastic appliance to date. He cut the bottom of a water bottle off, then worked at removing the ridges from where the cap screwed on top, so it could be modified to easily fit into a bottle that needed refilling. When he finished he left the funnel on the table and got his bike from off the wall. The troglodyte took his bike to the toll road and rode in between the booths for a couple of hours. While riding he made no unnatural movements and focused on himself rather than the cars passing by. If a car wanted to pass him, and there was traffic on the other side, the troglodyte had no problem with holding a line behind him on that ride. He enjoyed seeing the people who had been postponed momentarily drive off like they needed to, or even could, make up for lost time.

    He would read the bumper stickers on the cars that passed after the leader, and were made to go a little slower. The troglodyte's favorite one was, baby on board. As if the baby had agreed to put themselves in a metal box and be transported at high speeds. With a driver that would only pay the minimal amount of attention to the road. In order that they keep their infant pacified during the whole ordeal. Believing their sticker would make other drivers extra careful for their own lack there of. The troglodyte, although he didn't know it at the time, was training himself to not react to the honking of the horns. After a while, the troglodyte started to think of the horns on the road similarly to those of the post office parking lot. Not necessarily always beeping to him, they could be honking to one another.

The chain fell off his bike during the ride. He had to get way off the road to try to fix it. He didn't have any markers with him to alert the cars driving by of his whereabouts, so found a stick and drove it into the ground, to hang his shirt from. When the troglodyte had gotten the chain back on the bike and was heading back to the road, a car pulled over and asked the troglodyte if he needed any help. The troglodyte said they were all set now but accepted the lift the driver offered. The driver was going in the direction of the farm and told the troglodyte they were a business person who was interested in the surrounding land around the toll road. The driver said that there was great opportunity for growth on this newly found plot of land. They hoped to get a foot in the door before the foundation was laid. The troglodyte didn't talk much on the ride and allowed the driver to prophesy about all the great companies that were set for expansion.

When the driver pulled up to the distant toll booth, the troglodyte raised himself up from his seat, squatting in the car to see what the inside of that booth looked like. The driver paid the attendant and the troglodyte got his first look at the gate opening from a car's perspective. He fell back into his seat. A little farther down the road the troglodyte asked the driver to stop. He got his bike from the back of the vehicle. The driver handed the troglodyte a business card, and said that if he was ever interested in buying or selling land, the troglodyte should call them. The troglodyte shut the car door lackadaisically after hearing this, and had to reopen it so it would shut proper.

He mounted his bike and drove it through the farmer's fields, rather than the gravel which reminded the troglodyte off a skin deep wound or a bald head. When the troglodyte got to where the cows were grazing, he slowed down to not disturb them, before trying to pester them when they appeared too nonchalant. He couldn't get a rise out of any of the cows and wasn't able to incite any of the rage that was known to be toxic to humans. Just as a pig can become a boar if let into the wild, a cow can become a bull if it is continually made to be mad. The troglodyte had no luck inoculating the disease and cycled over to where the goats were. The goats were more active than the cows and the troglodyte tried not to disturb them.

The goats approached the troglodyte when they saw him though, and pleaded while they bleated for any food he might have. The troglodyte offered them a closed hand, only to disappoint them when he opened it, revealing it empty. He was trying to get his hand close enough to their head so that he could ring their bell. Goats who were not yet privy to the troglodyte's game, would look in the direction of the sounded bell and follow, hoping they may also be fed. When the goats were no longer interested in discovering the contents of the troglodyte's closed hand, he walked the rest of the way to the farm house, guiding his bike with the one and keeping the other as it was. The chicken coops were nearby, closer to the farm house, and the troglodyte decided it would be disrespectful not to pay them a visit as well. The troglodyte wasn't able to think of anything to do while around the chickens and freed himself from the overpowering smell that was polluting his thoughts.

The troglodyte knocked on the farmer's door. The son answered and was asked when the last time the coops were clean. The boy said that he cleaned them everyday and that his work was discussed throughout huge patches of the farming community. If the troglodyte were to believe what the child said was true, he had no desire to visit any less well maintained farms. He had no desire to talk with any of their overseers. If what was said was true, then the troglodyte was glad for the warning.

The troglodyte asked what the boy thought of the new toll road, which was something the boy had been yearning to talk about. He hadn't been able to for lack of receptive audience. When the boy tried to talk to his father about the road, he was unable to get a word in once the flood gates were opened. His sister couldn't be bothered. His mother would tell the boy he'd understand when he was older. She was raising him that way.

The boy didn't understand why a road, that essentially went nowhere, should require a toll to drive on it. The boy understood the revenue brought in by booths on busier roads, but couldn't find a reason for one on the road less traveled. The troglodyte admitted that he may in part be to blame, and that since he wasn't a member of either of the towns, taxes had to be collected for making use of his property. The farmer should also see some of the money by this reasoning, and the troglodyte hoped the information would calm the boy. The boy asked if the booths were temporary, fearing it would take a certain amount of time for the troglodyte and farmer to recoup their losses. The troglodyte didn't have an answer.

The farmer's wife entered the room and relayed hopes that the boy hadn't been troubling the troglodyte. The troglodyte assured the wife he hadn't and that she was raising a great thinker. The farmer's wife asked for the boy to go help the farmer,then sat across from the troglodyte and offered refreshments. The troglodyte told her that he was passing through. He ventured to ask why her son was so against the new toll road. She explained that the family would sit down each night to play a board game, and the boy's recent losing streak may be the source of his discontent.

The game was played when, each player chose a piece of farm equipment and took turns rolling dice to make their way across the board. With certain spaces that were landed on, the player would be able to receive fake money for doing various chores. Helping out their neighbors. On other spots the player would have the option of buying the property they now occupied, taxing any future player who lands on it. Spots that had been visited and had paid out the player, would change into spots available to purchase, after the player frequented it and the well had run dry. The object of the game was to occupy more territory than your opponent. Players who held on to their money without investing, at the end of the game would have to choose from the what if pile of cards. So that they may see what might have been had they only played the game.

The woman explained that the loser of the game was tasked with cleaning the chicken coop the next day. The boy had recently stopped trying to win at the game and was only going through the motions, settling that he would have to do an extra chore. The troglodyte asked why they didn't change the rules of the game or have a different punishment for the loser. The woman said that it was probably too late. Any rule changes done strictly on the boy's behalf would infuriate his sister, and the wife didn't want to damage her other child by trying to reverse the damage done to it's sibling. The troglodyte said that if she did decide to change the rules, the player with the most money halfway through the game could meet an early demise. Not so early that they didn't prepare, and gift their money by way of inheritance to a player, or players, of their choosing. The troglodyte said to not worry about the undercurrent message of mortality. The children were already used to seeing farm equipment break.

When the player resumes the game penniless, they can either revert back to their old ways, becoming a miser with their money, or turn over a new leaf to become a business mogul. They may wish to reenter the game just to play the villain, going after the handed outs. When she asked the troglodyte to explain how his rules would help the boy come to grips with some roads in life being tolling, he said he wasn't sure, but at least with his changes there would never be a definite loser. If they only played halfway through and didn't return penniless, no one could honestly say that they hadn't won. When the game was half done, the obvious loser would shed their title, once they gifted their imaginary titles to a beneficiary. The woman said she'd consider changing the rules, but not because of him, and asked why the troglodyte had come to visit the farm that day. The troglodyte said he didn't think he needed a reason to visit. It sounded hypocritical when he heard it. He demanded everyone else have a reason when they visited him.

The wife told the troglodyte she hadn't yet used the new road and wanted to know how it was. The troglodyte said that it was fine for walking or biking. Taking a vehicle on it could really test your patience. The troglodyte and the woman talked some more, about bringing the cows back home and different strategies for the board game, before the troglodyte finished the refreshments offered and got up to leave. The farmer's wife asked if the troglodyte would be leaving the farm with a souvenir like he had in the past. He asked what she had in mind. She got up from her seat and went to the closet to rummage around for a bit. When she returned she was holding a solid wooden box with two rows of craters spaced evenly apart. In each hole were semi flat marbles and the woman explained how to play the game. She said it was a good game, that he would be able to play even if there were no one around to face him. The troglodyte thanked her for the gift and asked for a bag to carry it in before leaving.

He put the bag around the handlebars of his bike and rode into the other town. He found a diner and parked his bike outside. He brought the game in with him. He alerted everyone at the diner of his arrival by the bells on the door, and worked to get the bag loose of the handle. When he was finally free to choose a seat, he saw they were almost all occupied by personal belongings of the diners. He found a booth near the window. When the waitress came around, he asked if the spot he picked was okay. She said she'd bring his order on a few smaller plates instead of one big one, to make the atmosphere around him seem more inviting, and asked what he would have. The troglodyte said he wanted whatever was considered local cuisine, so long as it wasn't beef, chicken or lamb. When the waitress returned to the table she had a tray of plates. She spread said plates out so the booth looked a little more as it should. The troglodyte invited the waitress to sit with him for a while, to tell him about her work life. She declined, telling him she had to get back to it.

The troglodyte left most of his food untouched and requested that it be bagged. It would be easier to bring it home that way. The diner said they still expected a tip, and didn't put the food in a bag until the troglodyte made good on the promise he was trying to make. Paying them before receiving his goods. The troglodyte returned to his bike without any more run-ins with the door, put each bag on the handlebars, and took the long way home.

When he got to his property he put the food in the fridge. The game on the workbench. He practiced palming the marbles once he had played the game a few times through. He wasn't interested in gambling at the time but figured that in the future things might be different. After playing a few more games, now with his added advantage, his mind turned to solitaire. The troglodyte went down into the basement of his house.

The troglodyte hadn't been in the basement for anything other than cases of water and non perishables, and had no real semblance of what was down there. He moved boxes around aimlessly, sometimes checking them before stacking new ones on top. Other times not. He knocked over one box. Inside were old photographs of landscapes, now splayed out on the floor. The troglodyte thought they must have belonged to the previous owner. He did have a camera but had no use for it. He wasn't planning on sharing pictures with anyone. Even if the troglodyte had been to the places where the photos were taken, he couldn't have taken them because he had no eye for beauty. The troglodyte found a few decks of cards at the bottom of one of the boxes. He didn't mind looking through any of the boxes that hadn't been taped shut. He took one of the decks with him back upstairs and left the basement as it was. A mess, but more or less his own.

The troglodyte set up the game of solitaire and prepared himself for a long night. He knew that solitaire was a numbers game. If he was able to win more times than draw he could consider it a success. He kept tally of his tally with the marbles from his other game. He lost some of those marbles when he jerked himself awake, after realizing he'd fallen asleep. It took a while for the troglodyte to trust his ears, but he eventually responded to the honk outside of his house. He picked the marbles up from off the floor, and with a full head of steam went outside to see what the problem was.

②5

    The postal worker was standing over the mail chute.
Nothing new. Then, they told the troglodyte what he was
asking of them was next to impossible. The troglodyte asked
if the postal worker had any suggestions for how to improve
on his design. He shot each one down for minor flaws in
their practicality. The troglodyte said that the mail chute
would stay as it was. It was suggested that the postal worker
take their vehicle off the road. They could throw the
newspaper at the troglodyte's house when they were close
enough. The troglodyte tried to make a joke about the postal
worker not being able to hurt the house's feelings. The
punchline went right to the gutter and over the postal
worker's head. The postal worker said they would do their
best to deliver the paper. They told the troglodyte he looked
like the type who may enjoy going to the post office, and if
he went there may have more luck.

    ...

    The troglodyte took the paper over to the toll booth
attendant and asked her what she had done with her time off.
She accepted the paper, and began to flip through it in
between customers. The troglodyte noticed she wasn't using
the coin carrier he had made for her and asked if it was
functioning properly. She assured him it was, and after
providing a demonstration said she just couldn't manage the
multitasking it required. She was able to use the coin carrier
if the driver requested to buy a plastic water bottle, but was
unable to justify using it when the customers asked that their
bottles be refilled. The troglodyte went back to the house to
grab the funnel. If the troglodyte is productive, everyone is
productive. After testing the funnel out with some new
customers, using the register for change, she tried to work

the coin carrier in to the equation. She was unable. She apologized to the troglodyte for not being able to make good use of his invention, and gave him all the recyclables from the booth. The troglodyte took his spoil back to the house, after asking if there was anything interesting in the paper.

He threw the recyclables near the workbench, not having found any inspiration for them yet, and began to move the furniture around his house. He took down all the chairs and objects that were stacked by his back door. He began to make clutter for his previously open floor plan. He put the chairs in the center of the room, circling a table that was not yet there. Any small desks, and foldable or collapsible chairs, were set up against the walls. Serving as mock booths. He put the deck of cards near the front door on the workbench. The box was left open and a few cards were sticking out. He cleaned the bathroom and checked the medicine cabinet for anything he may need to stock up on. He double checked the contents of the first aid kit. He opened the notebook he was transcribing into and tore a clean sheet of paper from the back. So that he could keep a list.

When his list was made, he wandered into the basement to look for material. He decided that even if he were to find what he was looking for, it would probably be just as easy to go to the store and get it. The troglodyte left his bicycle at his property and asked the toll booth attendant where he could find the supplies. When he had his answer he headed to the gas station.

When the troglodyte walked into the gas station, he thought he had made a mistake and stumbled into a smoke shop. The owner of the gas station dissuaded his fears though, greeting the troglodyte and smiling from ear to ear. The owner said that business had never been better, thanks to the troglodyte, and started to elaborate. Even though the gas station couldn't technically sell tobacco, the increased foot traffic had greatly helped out the business. At first all the tobacco stayed on the shelves and was asked about by many a customer. Then, some customers began to give their own suggestions to the owner, and all parties discovered that although the tobacco couldn't be sold, it could be gifted. If a buyer agrees to a price, the seller can mark up the non tobacco products to cover the cost of doing business. As long as the customer didn't say they bought the tobacco, and spoke obscurely, perhaps saying where they found some, word would spread about the gas station. Those who heard the rumors straight from the horse's mouth would venture to the gas station with some extra money. Those who heard it through the grapevine would go to the station expecting free product.

Either way, the foot traffic would continue to increase. The owner said that if he should run in to problems in the future, and be shaken down for a license, he would have enough money to pay the fine, make the initial investment, and still pay the required taxes thereafter. When the owner was done with their story, and the troglodyte had told him what he wanted to hear, he asked where he could find the medical supplies. He gave the owner his list. The owner went behind the counter and got the troglodyte what he needed. He practically threw the supplies at the troglodyte, and said they were a gift. The troglodyte left the gas station. He hoped the line the owner was walking wasn't as fine as it appeared to be.

The troglodyte took his shopping bag and headed to a mechanic's garage, where he saw a few used cars for sale in the lot. The troglodyte approached the secretary and asked

what kind of car they drove. In the same breath, if it had
given her any trouble. The woman said she wasn't the person
to talk cars with and suggested he try one of the mechanics.
The troglodyte asked what the right topic would be to talk
about with her. She said you darling, and asked the
troglodyte what days he was free. She would do everything
in her power to pencil him in, so the troglodyte went into the
garage to ask about the cars out front.

One of the mechanics who wasn't too busy, walked up to
the troglodyte and asked what it would take for him to drive
off the lot today. He answered his own question, and said
one of our cars. The troglodyte said he hadn't driven in more
than thirty years. That it would probably take more than what
the mechanic was able to offer. Unless, he drove him to the
registry and also got him some insurance. When the
mechanic understood the troglodyte had neither a car in the
shop, nor the ability to drive a new one home, he asked for
what reason the troglodyte was there. The troglodyte said
that he wanted to take a test drive. He emptied the contents
of the bag on the floor in between him and the mechanic.
The mechanic wasn't sure whether to applaud the
troglodyte's attempt at preparedness or be afraid for his
safety. He allowed the troglodyte rein of one of the cars. The
one that had a acquired a reserved spot in the lot.

He showed the troglodyte to the car, handed him the
keys, and asked what the last thing he remembered about
driving was. The troglodyte made it safely out of the lot, and,
to the mechanics relief, proved to be a decent driver. The
mechanic wanted to know what it was that made the
troglodyte give up driving in the first place. The troglodyte
was too focused on the road to hear. The mechanic tried
other small observations and inquiries, talking to himself the

whole while he was along for the ride. The troglodyte broke his silence when he asked the mechanic if he wanted the car gassed up. The mechanic said that a car runs better on a full tank. He emptied the ash tray in the car and told the troglodyte he wouldn't be able to pay at the pump.

The troglodyte pulled into the same gas station he'd been at earlier, coming dangerously close to hitting the pump, remembering wrongly that the hose was unnecessarily short. The mechanic offered to pump the gas. He promised the troglodyte he never would have done so, had the gas station a garage attached to it. The troglodyte went inside to pay. The owner was surprised to see the troglodyte back so soon. He looked over the troglodyte's shoulder to see if he was taking the piss out of him. He saw the car the troglodyte was driving and asked if he was planning on buying it. The troglodyte said he was not. The owner refused to believe him. He told him that the gas would also be free, since he was going to be making such a big purchase.

The troglodyte left the money for gas on the counter, and didn't bother arguing with the owner who was pleading for him not to do so. The mechanic asked for the change when the troglodyte had sat back in the driver's seat. The troglodyte said the owner was stubborn and wouldn't offer any. The mechanic, furious he had been short changed, went into the gas station to confront the owner. When he came back to the car, he told the troglodyte that the owner had offered to give all the money back, not just the change. Something about an apology for the poor service. The troglodyte let the mechanic have his narrative. He drove back to the garage, as silent as before. The mechanic talked as if he had just found money in his pocket.

The mechanic told the troglodyte to leave the car in front of the garage. He would have to put it back on display later. The mechanic laid on all plausible praise possible for the troglodyte. He tried to impress on him the importance of having a vehicle, and all the opportunities that come with it. The troglodyte thanked the mechanic before walking away from the garage. An anomaly to all that passed him. The troglodyte was in such a mood for travel, that he took a hack to the nearest lake not within walking distance, which was a broad scope, and looked for any docks that were very well maintained. He found a boat rental outfit, and when asked what they could do to get him in a boat today, replied an invitation was all he needed.

He went out on the water with some captain and three other people. Two made a couple and one was a stranger, as was he. The captain pointed things out while they were cruising, to which the passengers ravenously took pictures. The person who was travelling alone offered to share their camera with the troglodyte. So that he may feel more part of the experience. The troglodyte didn't follow their logic, and had no intentions of working for free in his leisure time. When the shore was no longer visible, the captain produced a half dozen fishing rods. He set theirs lines with bait. He cast.

The couple had brought food. The party ate while the boat was stagnant, with hopes that the fishing lines would soon be taut. The troglodyte was the first one to get a bite, or so was told by the captain, who had control of all the lines but told the passengers which one belonged to whom. When the captain reeled the fish out of the water, he had the troglodyte hold it while pictures were taken. He asked the troglodyte how he felt at that moment. The troglodyte asked if they were the ones fishing or being fished. He didn't tip the captain very much when they returned to shore.

The troglodyte walked back to his house after his busy day. He heard a plane fly overhead. As it got closer, the troglodyte felt anxious and wondered about the irrational feeling. He had no reason to fear the plane, but when noises would crescendo so would his stomach. He stocked his medicine cabinet when he was inside, listening for the sound of the plane to fade in the distance. The troglodyte didn't do much after that. Eating when he had to. Preparing for sleep before he had to. He slept through the night. He dreamed he was running through a field, chased by a plane piloted by the mechanic. Painted on the side of the plane was a participation trophy. He wasn't an oneironaut and had no control of where his mind went. The troglodyte didn't try to make sense of the dream when he woke. His attention was already on the day ahead of him. Something that the newspaper delivery was conditioning him to do.

He looked out one of his windows at the mail ditch. The troglodyte thought it a good sign that the postal worker wasn't there. He prepared to go outside to search for signs that they'd been around. It was a bit of a blustery day, so the troglodyte grabbed his goggles and even his vest. So as to not get pelted by wayward unturned stones exiting his house. Because of the wind and it's path of inclusion, the troglodyte was not able to make out any tire tracks, which would have now been covered with twigs and rocks. He walked to the back of the house and found the newspaper resting in one of his collapsible chairs. The troglodyte was glad that the postal worker had taken the initiative in delivering the paper. He read the headlines as he went about his duty as middleman.

When the attendant saw what the troglodyte was wearing, she told him about their water bottling enterprise. She kept saying, but, before, supply wasn't able to meet demand, and after anything that wasn't that. Since she couldn't leave the toll booth, she had no way of telling the troglodyte when she was running low on inventory. When she disclosed the figures to the troglodyte, he promised he would find a way to make it work. He handed her the paper. She skimmed the tags, reciting under her breath, until she appeared to have found something interesting, and read silently. When she looked up from the paper, the troglodyte was walking away from the booth. Making calculations in his head and displaying them on his hands. He returned with three cases of water. Dragging them in a wagon that didn't seem to fit him, and said that that should be enough water for the rest of the day. She agreed, and took the cases the troglodyte slid through the window less used. Their conversation ended when they began discussing things they thought the other person might want to talk about. Since neither of them wanted to talk any more, the answers were short and the questions profound.

The troglodyte went into town intent on checking in with the barber. His business. Before the troglodyte got to the barbershop, he saw his idea had come to life, and studied the distorted reflection staring back at him. He wasn't sure if he felt any more enticed to get a haircut, but realizing that he wasn't the average customer, didn't give his thought much weight. He passed two more of the rotating mirrors before seeing the good old fashioned. When the troglodyte entered the barbershop, the room became quiet and all heads turned to the barber who was in mid cut. The barber put the scissors on the counter and turning to the troglodyte, told him he had a lot of nerve coming in there. The barber paused for dramatic effect, allowing the troglodyte to prepare for rejection, before breaking into a smile. He told the troglodyte he should have let them know he was coming so they could have prepared a royal welcome. At this, the rest of the barbers and the customers cheered the troglodyte. Even attempting to start a chant, but not finding a characteristic of the troglodyte they could all agree on for his title. He was nameless to them.

The troglodyte was once again happy for the business owner he had been able to help. However, he thought they may be giving him too much credit and themselves not enough. Increasing foot traffic was one thing, but without their superior service or product, the troglodyte would only be inciting mobs. The barber asked the troglodyte if his plastic accessories were also part of some grand marketing scheme. Whether or not the troglodyte could divulge any of those secrets. The troglodyte said he hadn't found an application for his plastic ware yet, but would share any ideas if he stumbled across one. The barber offered the troglodyte a shave, and when done, shew the troglodyte his work in a improved mirror. He was able to get it at a discount because of the ask of his order. The troglodyte told the barber he was satisfied, and took off the goggles and vest to shake them free of any hair. The troglodyte left the barbershop following the advertisement in reverse. Once free of the mirrors he thought there was something lacking.

He knew that the pleased customers would likely want to spend even more money after making improvements to their appearance. He saw that where the signs stopped were no shops of any kind. The troglodyte followed all the other possible routes branching off of the spinning mirrors. He discovered much of the same with every case. The troglodyte thought that more signs needed to be upped. Just like how the barbershop had done. So clientele could be led to client based businesses by varying degrees of subliminal messaging.

②6

The troglodyte went to the diner. He asked the waitress if she noticed anything different about him. The waitress said he looked familiar, so he must have done something to his appearance. The troglodyte told her how he had been walking along the street going about his day, when the glare off of what he thought to be a window struck his eye. Upon closer examination, by means of getting closer to the glare, without looking directly at it, he noticed that it was actually a mirror that roused his attention. He wouldn't have looked twice, had it not been spinning in the fashion of a barber pole. He walked to the end of the street, turned a corner, and saw another of the same devices. He didn't have to look twice. It was the same. He followed the trail until he got to an actual barbershop, complete with red and white barber pole, and had himself a shave. The waitress said there definitely was something different about him. She wasn't sure that that was it.

The troglodyte went on and asked the waitress how the diner marketed its existence. The waitress said that was above her pay grade and ran off into the kitchen. The troglodyte was left with his thoughts just long enough to start to wonder if he had offended the waitress. He was saved an answer, when a manager sat across from him. They introduced themself with a long list of titles, head of research and development among them. The manager asked the troglodyte what good will he offered to the diner. The troglodyte answered without hesitation, letting the manager know it would be done for free. The troglodyte laid out his plan of copying the barbershops strategy, with as few changes as possible.

The troglodyte thought that over marketing with food was dangerous. He cautioned their approach shouldn't contain any images of food on the signs. If a would be customer saw too many images of food they would start to become creative with their choices, and may head to the market to pick up ingredients for their perfect meal. If the customer was not so outgoing, they may stop and settle with the last advertisement they saw. They could rehash the list of logos and choose the best compromise. The troglodyte proposed the advertisement be a different reminder telling them they want to eat. Signs showing physical activity or strenuous exercise. The troglodyte thought that his tactic would appeal to a wide demographic. The people who had put in a hard day at work would understand the diner could provide all the sustenance needed for the day ahead. Those who had not done a hard day's work would tell themselves they had, and were deserving. The people who were opposed to difficult physical activity would also head to the diner. Comforted in their thoughts that they prefer the lifestyle they chose and ate as such.

The manager liked the idea as much as they would let on, and asked if the troglodyte would be providing the signage. If he would be steering the marketing campaign, but the troglodyte had already gotten up to leave the diner. The manager asked where he was going. The troglodyte said his work was not yet finished. He said something under his breath about future endeavors.

. . .

After the troglodyte dashed out of the diner, he went to the train station to see if he couldn't make one last impression in the day. When he got to the station the first thing he did was head to the food court. Where he waited for the sky to open up so he could have a dessert. When he got to the front of the line and received his order with a smile, the troglodyte tipped generously, saying their establishment was the cornerstone of any good food court. The cashier said she appreciated the troglodyte's input. She asked if he'd like to fill out a feedback form. With just ten minutes of his time he could make or break their food safety rating. Possibly draw in more business. The troglodyte replied that when he was finished with the dessert, if he still felt the same way he would do so. He took the treat back to a table with one of the chain's logos on an umbrella overhead. The troglodyte closed the umbrella when he sat down, hoping by doing so he could recreate the feeling of eating outside. After all, he had just got a treat from an ice cream cart. A little different than the company's logo, but overpriced just the same.

The troglodyte overheard a conversation taking place nearby. Breaking him out of his food coma. Allowing him to focus on anything other than the sensations of eating, which served no practical purpose once aware that the food was edible. A man and woman were arguing, and by the amount of time between completed thoughts, the troglodyte knew the argument must be reaching a close. At the beginning of the argument both parties were able to clearly state their point of view, without interruption, even if the other person was thinking about what they would say next. Before they got the chance. Rather than listen to the possibly opposing opinion. As the conversation became more heated, the person who was supposed to be listening would start to break through. They would no longer pay respect by waiting for their counterpart to finish, and feel proud of what they had to say until the moment it left their mouth, and they blurted out what they thought couldn't wait. When the argument was over, and only the parties involved knew who won, the troglodyte crowned the victor himself. He approached the table, making sure to maintain eye contact with his esteemed as he sidled over.

He didn't want to appear weak in the eyes of the orator and sat down without first being asked. The couple asked the troglodyte why he sat down. He replied humans were given knees so that legs would bend for a chair, and said he needed to take a load off. Hearing this, the man and woman's eyes both began to tear up and they attempted to start yelling at one another again. The troglodyte did his best to calm them, and asked if it was something he said. The woman and man both apologized to the troglodyte for their behavior. The woman said that her and the man were going through a custody battle over their adolescent child.

The man said that while they were in court they were not allowed to take up harsh tones in front of the judge. So they compromised and decided that anything that they couldn't say in court, they could get out at each other in a public place. They had chosen the food court because people typically didn't spend a lot of time hanging around there once done eating. This allowed for the couple to air all their grievances without fear of being disturbed or reported. As ideal as the food court was a spot for them to get in a shouting match, it was even better that they were in a train station. Where strangers put their lives on hold and are reborn in a place they need to be. The troglodyte asked whether more progress was made in court or otherwise. The man said that if they didn't get out all their frustrations they would most likely be arrested in the presence of the judge. The troglodyte said civility is the right approach for some situations. Definitely not in matters concerning flesh and blood. The troglodyte could understand why the primal instincts kicked in when they discussed their child. The troglodyte left their table after his remark and went back to his own. He reopened the ice cream cart logo and left the food court. Signaling to any others that that table was now in business.

The troglodyte approached one of the tellers and didn't recognize them as someone who had served him previously. He asked to speak with their manager but was denied until he provided a good enough reason for her to close down the window for a non paying customer. The troglodyte said if she checked her computer, she would find a ticket being held for him by the station. He said sorry she didn't get the commission. She asked for his information. He told her to look through the system for any tickets that were being held for people that hadn't provided information. She told him she didn't think there was a standard practice of separating tickets for nameless people, but checked anyway. She reported to the troglodyte she couldn't find anything identifiable. The troglodyte told her that they must have sent the ticket to his house then, and asked to see the manager once again. She said she could do the troglodyte one better, and told how there was a management training class he could sign up for. So that the troglodyte could help with the train station economy, since he didn't want to buy a ticket.

The troglodyte took this to mean that there was no manager currently at the train station. He left the teller's window and walked with his thoughts. If he became a manager then he would have to put all his eggs in one basket, and only be able to look out for himself. The idea that he was hoping to propose to the train station manager was a marketing scheme that would involve more subliminal messaging. The troglodyte thought that the train station could bring in more customers by showing exotic places, that looked familiar, in their marketing campaign. His plan was to doctor a picture taken on a street that someone walking would have had to pass a few streets back. The image would be put on the street they were currently walking. The picture of the street they had previously been on would look different because of alterations made, and would appear tropical or wintry depending on the destination the station was trying to market. The troglodyte thought that by showing the altered picture, people would have the urge to travel and get away. They would be comfortable with the purchase because of the connection they made with the street.

When the troglodyte got back to his house he went straight into the basement. To look for the box of old photographs. He took a handful of them out to study, and see if any of the pictures were of the town. He found a few that could pass as the streets nearby the train station. He thought the grainy film would only make the process of superimposing a background easier. He brought the photos up from the basement and left them on the workbench. He figured the best course of action would be to take it upon himself to change the images and mail them to some higher up of the transit authority. Using his three colored markers he did his best to make the photos look convincing, before deciding he would add a note with the drawings, and allowed his artistic ability to be compromised. He added trees that looked out of place, sea shore where there had been none, and a blistering red sun to every picture. He traced the original picture with pencil once done with the additions, making it easy to see improvements, and wrote his letter. In the letter he explained the purpose of the photos and his idea for the marketing campaign. He signed next to the word intention, and wrote he wanted to help out a fellow traveling salesman. He didn't have the right sized envelope for the pictures, or an address to send them to, so made a plan to head to the post office the next morning. He hoped they would have both. When he was finally ready, he fell asleep very quickly.

7

The troglodyte woke and went about his house, doing
what he was becoming accustomed to doing in the morning.
He found the newspaper and surveyed the area around his
backyard. He hadn't noticed it the previous day, but the rope
was no longer snaking around the reflectors and must have
caught onto the mail truck. Some reflectors were pulled out
of the ground, having been caught on the rope, while most of
the quills were no longer standing. A few of the reflectors
were broken, those unlucky enough to have been in the mail
truck's path, but now that a route had been established the
troglodyte didn't expect to see any more damage. He took
the paper to the attendant, who asked a favor of him as soon
as he was close enough to do so. She explained to the
troglodyte that the water bottles were flying out of the cases
and business was good, but she had to imposition him. She
needed to use his restroom. The troglodyte told her he'd
show her the way to his house. She said he would have to
stay in the booth and cover for her. The troglodyte told her
he wasn't ready for the responsibility. She promised it would
only be a couple minutes and he may not even have any
customers.

She left the toll booth, leaving the door open for the
troglodyte, and found her way to the troglodyte's house. The
troglodyte entered the booth and left the door open, so that
he wouldn't feel trapped, and looked around. Underneath the
register was a box of what the troglodyte assumed were the
night attendant's belongings, and an empty box beside,
which must be the home away from home of the day
attendant's decorations. The troglodyte saw the funnel right
by the customer window and the cases of water. He noticed
all the empty water bottles were beginning to pile up, having

assumed most of the space on the floor. A customer pulled up to the window and after receiving their change, asked the troglodyte where the regular attendant was. The troglodyte, having not prepared to be taking the attendant's place, had not worn his plastic vest and was embarrassed the transaction had not went smoothly. The troglodyte told the driver that the attendant had to step out to use the restroom, to which the driver said they could use a restroom around here as well.

The troglodyte knew he shouldn't make the offer, but found himself doing so anyway, and told the driver if they got off the toll road and parked, the troglodyte could show them to his house. Where there they could use his facility. The attendant came back to the booth before the driver could answer, and asked the troglodyte if there was a problem. The troglodyte gave the driver a water bottle and the customer drove off slowly down the toll road, trying to find any place to park so they wouldn't have to double back and park in the attendant's lot. The attendant resumed her position in the toll booth. She thanked the troglodyte for his hospitality. The troglodyte said she was welcome to use his place whenever she needed, her name was connected to the property just as much as his.

The troglodyte returned to his house and locked all the windows and doors. The windows locked normally. He used a knife to unscrew the door knobs and positioned them so they would lock towards the outside. He now planned on going into the town and didn't want to risk the driver using his place while he was gone. He took his bike, the photos and their duplicates, and his letter to the post office, and waited to be called. When he got to the front of the line, the clerk sold him the proper sized envelope. Told him he would need a court order to get the address from them. The troglodyte asked why there was such a need for secrecy. The clerk told him that there is a firm stance concerning moving trains. The troglodyte gave the envelope its contents, and headed to the police station to try to find the proper channels.

The constable who greeted the troglodyte at the front desk, recognized him for the man who wanted a free ride and asked about the troglodyte's well being. The troglodyte said he was looking for the address of the head office for the local train station, or a nudge in that direction. The constable looked at the troglodyte from over his glasses. He wrote something down into his notebook and underlined it a few times. He gave the troglodyte the address, wrote something more in his notes, then told the troglodyte the needed to use the address responsibly. Saying this, he wrote, gave warning, down in his notes. The troglodyte thanked the constable and returned to the post office to send his letter.

Upon seeing the envelope with the proper address, the clerk, who could verify that it was correct due to her curiosity once the troglodyte left, asked how he had produced it. She was relieved when the troglodyte told her that it had been given to him by the authorities, which removed her from suspicion. She let the wind out of the troglodyte's sails when she informed that he couldn't send the mail to that address, because they were on a do not mail list. The troglodyte argued his case. The clerk was unable to help him and apologized on behalf of the post office.

Since the troglodyte couldn't mail the package to the address he was given, and since no officials of the transit system would speak to him, he decided just to leave it anywhere in the station. Hoping some lowly employee would think it their ticket to a higher position, and return the package to the address on the envelope. Proving themselves trustworthy, and able to take initiative, to the higher up with the supposed missing item. The troglodyte left the train station empty handed and thought that if it was meant to be, the envelope would find it's way back to him. He would be able to discuss strategy with whoever found him, by way of it. The troglodyte went back to his house to collect his own missing item. The ticket that the station must have sent, for he was no longer in the system. He checked the mail chute and found the ticket close enough to his side that he needn't use the bellows. The ticket was dated for departure in a few days. The troglodyte sat on the front steps of his house, and weighed the pros and cons of him taking a trip.

On the one hand, he hadn't left his surrounding area for more than thirty years. He may never get the chance again, knowing himself and the life cycle of his lifestyle. If he didn't go, he could stay around and continue to bear witness to the progress that was being made. If things stayed as they were, could even have a chance to relate all he observed. The troglodyte went about his house and took inventory of everything he had, basement included. Not expecting to find anything of value, he was not disappointed. He knew that he could leave the house and take his trip without having to worry about that. The troglodyte took the ticket to the day attendant, and asked if she would be interested in watching his house while he took the trip. She said she would have no problem doing so. She asked the troglodyte if he was going anywhere special. The troglodyte told her the name of the station he was heading for and the town it was in. She had never heard of either, and was excited for the troglodyte to live mysteriously.

...

When the day for the troglodyte's departure arrived, he brought with him to the station his plastic vest and goggles. All the money that he had stored in his house. He planned on returning to the house and trusted the attendant, but knew if he didn't take precautions, he would have to deal with his inner monologue talking up the consequences. He left the bellows with the mail chute, which he had torn out of the ground, in his back yard. He stocked the refrigerator with as many plastic water bottles as it could hold. He had removed one of the plastic reflectors from its post and put it on the outside of the door to his bathroom. He expected drivers would want to make use of his restroom since he had offered it before. He told the attendant that any drivers who did wish to make use of his facilities would have to be screened by her. Should she approve, her house being his house, she should treat them accordingly. Having officially placed the care of his place in the day attendant's hands, any more thoughts on the subject would be out of place, and were therefore out of his mind.

When he made it to a terminal where he could see the train arrive, he searched the surrounding waste baskets for any self affirmations for his recent thought pattern. No matter how minute the detail, if whatever he saw reminded him of something that had been in his mind the past few days, he could feel that unbecoming feeling of talking oneself into believing that they were finding other cogs that would help them become useful. The troglodyte didn't find anything while rummaging that surprised him at its relevance. He boarded the train when it came. Attaching himself to the other people who were also putting their lives on hold

②8

The troglodyte took a seat in one of the cars a few down from where he entered the train. The first cars he saw were already full of people. Otherwise the troglodyte wouldn't have made the extra effort of walking and scanning for seats. Since he was travelling alone and was unable to feel embarrassed by silence, if it were possible he would have sat in between just about anyone. Envied are those who can content themself to the luxury of sitting for the whole journey. The car that the troglodyte was sitting in was at about half capacity. It may have been so because of the people that appeared to be fighting some sort of sickness. Once the troglodyte had found his seat, he kept his head down. He could have sworn there were more people around him than there truly were, because of the different variations in the coughs and sneezes he heard. When the troglodyte had looked up and saw someone coughing terribly, he asked them what was the matter.

When the person had enough air in their lungs to give an answer, they told the troglodyte if he wasn't careful he was going to get it. The troglodyte questioned no more, not wanting to draw first blood, and allowed the person the space they needed. When one of the passengers got up and forgot their paper in the seat they left, the troglodyte looked around the train and tried to make eye contact with anyone else who may be trying to claim it. He mistook a challenger for someone who met his eyes before they had to sneeze. The troglodyte brought the paper back to his seat and read it the whole way through. When the troglodyte arrived at his destination, he closed the editorial section and took the rest of his possessions with him.

The train station that he stepped into had a similar layout to the one he had left, but appeared to have a central theme. The troglodyte went to the food court and was shocked to not find any of the food chain logos on the umbrellas. He went to one of the stands and ordered a plate. When the plate was clear, he left it on one of the tables with logo-less umbrella. So that above would be as below. He bused the surrounding tables for the same reason.

He turned around once outside, to make sure he had gotten off at the right place, then put his vest and goggles on so he could start exploring the town. Right away he noticed the people in the new town were much more outspoken about their thoughts on the troglodyte's appearance. He figured that the reason for this was, the new townspeople didn't know the troglodyte's backstory. Even though the troglodyte had no backstory in the other town, he at least thought they thought they knew why he did as he does. When the troglodyte had exhausted all the reasons he could come up with for his strange attire, he took off both articles. He put his hand through the vest and the goggles around his palm. He walked in this fashion, stopping for curious people for whom he brought life to the inanimate. A story arc was created for the dummy. He received some tips for his act from people who believed a show on the road was inherently better. During a quiet stretch of his walk, when no one asked of him to entertain, the troglodyte started to practice with the dummy. He asked it questions and spoke for it by answering himself. After a particularly gruelling self introspection, the troglodyte decided that the vest and goggles routine had run its course. He brought them to a river. The fish could decide on their own what they thought about aquariums in a very low risk way.

The troglodyte sat by the river and tried to figure out if it connected to the one he was familiar with. If it was the same one. Or if one was a river and the other something else. Having paid so little attention during the train ride and not wanting to look for his internal compass, he didn't get far. He watched his repurposed plastic float along, deciding to follow the path of the vest once it and the goggles had separated. He followed the route it would take and saw some kids down river who were playing with sticks by the shore. The troglodyte, intending the repurposed plastic to be used by fish, ran along the river and tried to get the attention of the children. They noticed him but didn't move from the shore. The troglodyte began yelling louder and throwing any loose change he had earned from his act behind him as he ran.

This got the children off their feet and soon they were running after him, unconcerned with the trash floating down the river. The troglodyte saw that his distraction had worked just in time, for he had run out of change to throw, and told the kids so once they caught up with him. They said that was what they were meaning to tell him. They asked if he wanted his money back. The troglodyte told them it wasn't his money entirely, but that his business partner had been asking him to hold on to it. Since he no longer had a partner, he no longer needed to hold on to it. The kids had caught him in the process of letting go. He said they could keep the money so long as they didn't mention where they got it. It was asked that they not go spreading rumors that there was money to be found by the river. The kids went back to the spot they were at before. The troglodyte followed the river back to where he received his last tip. From there he went in a new direction, away from the river and found a sunhat tending garden.

The troglodyte yelled over to the sunhat, though a quieter voice would have sufficed, and asked how the crop was this year. The sunhat looked up from their work, told the troglodyte it was too early in the season for such nonsense, and resumed working. The troglodyte rephrased his question and asked how much crop the sunhat was expecting, which fetched an even more biting answer. The troglodyte kept up his questioning, until all that was left for him to ask was if he could help with what the sunhat was doing. The sunhat said it was more of a one person job. The troglodyte didn't push his luck with the sunhat's hospitality. He walked away from the garden without taking anything or disturbing it further.

The troglodyte hadn't taken a vacation in a long time. It was understandable how he'd forgotten that not everyone he passed was a vacationer, or considered their home town any kind of vacation spot. There would be some people he met that found him enviable and would behave in a distasteful manner. Others wouldn't be able to stand the sight of him not working while they had to. The troglodyte wondered where he could congregate with the retired, the sabbatical takers, and the efficient types. Those who didn't have to work, but had probably chosen to at some point in their life. Where he may have chosen a park had he been in the familiar town, there he chose to follow the theme of the train station and headed to the beach.

When he got to the beach he took a towel that was hanging near the outside showers. He didn't sit far off. He wasn't an animal. He hoped that if he had grabbed someone's towel by mistake they would be able to recognize it nearby. If the towels were complimentary, then the troglodyte planned to return the towel, walking the length of the beach until he found a hamper. He couldn't return a used towel to the rack. The troglodyte watched the waves going in and out, and started to tire because of it. As the troglodyte's head slowly turned to the ground he noticed the designs on the towel. If the towel was in fact someone else's, and they couldn't get out of the shower to identify it, they would have a difficult time explaining the pattern to anyone trying to help them. The color scheme was such that some viewers may be more drawn to the bold colors, others would have an eye for the ambient. The troglodyte was not disturbed though as he sat on the beach. After watching what he assumed were the same flock of seagulls circling around him for the fourth time, he got up from the towel to look for a place it could be laundered.

The closest thing he found to what he was looking for, was a different outdoor shower on the other side of the beach. He folded the towel up, before putting it under one of the shower spouts, and turned on the water for half of a minute. He hoped the next person to see it would be more qualified than he and react appropriately. Since the troglodyte hadn't left anything at the other side of the beach, he stayed in the new part of town and entered a novelty t shirt shop. No one looked at him or showed any recognition when he entered. The staff were used to countless faceless faces and customers couldn't be bothered with other vacationers, whom they considered less than themselves. The troglodyte asked for help from one of the staff members, who was surprised something was asked of them while on the clock. They looked at the troglodyte for a while before sauntering towards him. When they were within earshot they informed the troglodyte about the deals they had on shirts, and asked if that answered his question. The troglodyte said it did, but wanted to know how the worker knew what he was going to ask. The worker had already turned away when they saw the troglodyte's eyes light up. They didn't trouble the troglodyte with a response.

The troglodyte bought a couple of t shirts, a pair of sunglasses and a towel. The same worker rang him up that had broken the news about the deals. When the troglodyte repeated his question, the worker said the answer had been written his face. The troglodyte tested the theory and asked the cashier a yes or no question and attempted to stow any expressions. The worker answered the troglodyte's question correctly and the troglodyte left the store.

If his face were so easily readable, the troglodyte wondered whether all of his interactions were effected and afflicted by it. The sunhat also probably knew all they needed to know within one second of looking at him, and may have been more friendly had the troglodyte been able to mask his intentions. Since the troglodyte did things differently than one would expect, the people he interacted with that assumed he would behave in a certain manner, when he did not had to confront their being wrong. They behaved differently themselves while in his presence. When a person such as the worker correctly assumes the troglodyte's intentions, the troglodyte then has to confront his own inner landscape and act accordingly. In this way, when the troglodyte was secluded his intentions were always infallible, but while in society the troglodyte must guess from one moment to the next. Next to the rest of us.

The troglodyte waited outside the t shirt shop for inspiration to strike, and not finding any, hailed a hack to take him to a place he could stow his possessions. The hack the troglodyte took, belonged to the same company as the other hacks the troglodyte had taken. He asked the driver how big of a company it was they worked for. The driver said they weren't sure. They asked the troglodyte whether he thought that bigger company employees make more than small company employees. The troglodyte said that since the big companies have more promotion, they probably are able to pay their workers better. Though since smaller companies have less people to pay, they may be able to compete through perks and bonuses.

The driver asked the troglodyte what business he was in. The troglodyte told the hack driver he was a recluse and didn't work for a living. The driver pulled over to the side of the road, looked back at the troglodyte, saw that he had shopping bags and continued with the fare. When the driver arrived in a part of town packed with hotels and motels, they told the troglodyte how much he owed and wished him luck. The troglodyte paid and reciprocated the well wishes. He told the driver that, big fish in a little pond and small fish in a big pond are both constrained by their imagination. The troglodyte slammed the car door. He felt a tug at his arm as he walked away. One of the shopping bags was in the process of unstucking itself from the door and had ripped open.

The troglodyte squatted down to pick up the towel that was now on the ground. He was hit by exhaust as the driver began to pull away. The troglodyte, upon gathering his bearings, stood up and shook his fist at the hack driver. He then looked for somewhere to stay. He picked the Sunnyside Up Motel and Grille, and paid for a three night accommodation. The clerk behind the desk asked where the troglodyte was travelling from. More importantly, if he was enjoying his time in their lovely little sea side town. The troglodyte did his best to explain his living situation to the clerk. The clerk had hoped for a simple answer, but did agree he found the people of the town a little standoffish. The clerk said that underneath their hard exterior was a soft and warm center. If the troglodyte should find any trouble he was always welcome back to the motel to escape himself. The clerk handed the troglodyte his key and a complimentary gift basket. The basket was reserved for customers who had chosen to stay three nights. The room was reserved for him.

The room was small in comparison to a hotel room. The troglodyte found it to be just the right size. He laid the towel on the bed, with the t shirts over the pillows, and went to sleep. From behind closed eyelids, the troglodyte saw wild scenarios happening at his house while he was away. He was saved from his delusions by a wake up call, one not requested but that he should have seen coming. The automated voice on the phone said, rise and shine, open your blinds, the sun is on its way; do not delay greeting the day, the hour is upon you. The troglodyte let the recording play through a number of times before hanging the phone up, not finding the message displeasing. He put on one of the novelty shirts, with the sunglasses, and headed for the motel office. He was to compliment the clerk on their establishment and its practices.

The clerk said that they didn't know who or what was responsible for the recording, and only knew to send it to certain rooms at certain times. The troglodyte asked why he had gotten a call even though one was not requested. The clerk explained that since he was taking a three day trip, they thought that the first day there should be a wake up call, so that the troglodyte can make the most of the time he had. The second and third days, the call would not be as important because the guest would have already had a chance to experience anything they so desired. On the first day. So would have planned for the upcoming days. Allowing for extra time to be had sleeping. The troglodyte found the clerk's explanation plausible, and asked what their guests usually did with the first day at the motel. The clerk said that every guest was different but they all shared in their disdain for disclosing much information to the clerk.

The troglodyte said he was sorry to hear it. He added, he wasn't a man with a very rich personal life so couldn't help the clerk either. The clerk said that when they had first moved to town, they spent their time relaxing. So the troglodyte asked why he would need a wake up call. The clerk said after they had done so much relaxing that it became stressful, they went to the carnival and entertained themself that way. The troglodyte hadn't been to a carnival since he was a child. He couldn't remember exactly what one was, so guessed he wouldn't like it now. He went with the clerk's first suggestion, and spent the day relaxing on the beach again. The troglodyte joined in on a game of frisbee when asked but couldn't figure out how to win. When his teammates all were cheering without him, he decided to leave.

The troglodyte walked the beach and looked for any sea shells or sea glass. When he would find some, he threw them back into the ocean, so that they wouldn't be left where he had already laid eyes on them. Which possibly would allow another person to find them easier. The troglodyte went in the ocean for a couple of hours at the end of the day, and once back at the motel, told the clerk about how he had felt while in the water. The clerk said they were kicking themself for not suggesting to the troglodyte that activity, but hadn't remembered not to forgot that the best things in life are free. Free things are often simple.

The troglodyte spent the night at the motel's pool, and the game room adjacent. Switching between the two when the other would became dull. He swapped stories with the people he played cards. He gave the people in the pool more than enough room to feel comfortable. One of the people sitting across from the card table had a toothpick in their mouth and was using it to gesticulate their thoughts and feelings. Rather than talking they would move the toothpick in different ways to convey consent and dissent. The troglodyte asked if the player had any extra toothpicks that they could part with. The troglodyte was offered a toothpick and practiced moving it around his mouth so that he wouldn't have to speak much more. The troglodyte ended the night at the card table so that any money he won wouldn't be stolen when he went in the pool. He left the game room with more than he had entered with.

The troglodyte took a nap for a few hours. Then checked out of the motel. Letting the clerk know what his plans for the day were. The clerk noticed the way the toothpick moved around the troglodyte's mouth when he wasn't talking, and asked the troglodyte if he had an extra one. The troglodyte said no. After he left the clerk did find a toothpick. Through practice, the clerk didn't once let the toothpick fall from his mouth while talking to any customers they saw that day. Nor any days after, until the new way to emote had become lackluster.

The troglodyte walked around the beach town. He felt more isolated than he had while living away from society. Here the people were cognizant of him but made it a point to act any other way. Even during long encounters he felt small.

The people weren't any less friendly towards each other, but the troglodyte felt that his treatment was different. So he made it a point to get in as many uncomfortable situations as possible. Doing nothing to resolve the awkwardness, instead welcoming it and letting it run its course. When the sun was beginning to set, the troglodyte headed for the train station and tried to gather any information pertinent to him getting back to his property. One of the clerks was able to find him a ticket, for a train that was leaving sooner rather than later. They handed him the ticket, and asked if he was travelling for business or pleasure. The troglodyte found the question odd to be asked at the end of their interaction, since he had noticed that people in the service industry do their best to fill the silence during the downtime. He answered his journey was for a little of both. The troglodyte found the terminal he was to wait at, and laid the beach towel on a bench. So he wouldn't have to use his hand to clear it of any debris. He waited for his train. The troglodyte boarded the train with thoughts on how short his trip seemed to have been. He was anxious to get back to his place, if only to get away from it sooner. The ride back to the troglodyte's favored train station seemed quicker than when he usually made his way there. The troglodyte soon exited that station.

9

The troglodyte went to the office to see if they had been expecting him in the past three days. If he had missed any appointments. The troglodyte entered the building through a side door that connected to the stairs so that he wouldn't need to walk through the first floor. He did stop on the secretary's floor and at her desk. She asked the troglodyte about the t-shirt he was wearing and had he been on a trip. The troglodyte told her about the beach. The strange sort of folk that had made it their habitat. He said the trip had been a welcome change of pace, until it became a reminder that he needed to change his pace. After that, he couldn't stand being there any longer and wanted to get back to his property to continue on his journey. The troglodyte gave the clerk one of the novelty shirts, which had a picture of a sand castle. The words wouldn't last as long as the sandcastle in the picture, and would be replaced next season. They said, my little place by the sea.

The troglodyte walked the length of the rest of the floor. He found a spot at the end of the line to wait for the council. He received no priority and was not called to the front. He didn't have to wait long though. The people in front of him either had their matters resolved quickly or had been corralled to appear at a later date. The council members all smiled in turn when they saw the troglodyte enter. The member on the left seeing him first and acknowledging, the other two following suit once suited. The troglodyte stated his reason for being there and asked if he was missed during his time away. The council said that they hadn't had anything scheduled for him but had received a landowner recently who had asked about the troglodyte property.

The council hadn't provided the interested party with any information since the troglodyte's house wasn't a part of the town. They had told the person if they stuck around the troglodyte's place for long enough they were bound to see him. The troglodyte didn't vocalize his wonderment at why policy makers and law upholders would send a stranger to someones property, and give them hospitality when it was not theirs to give. instead thanking the council and informing them he didn't expect to be hosting them at his place anytime soon. The council members had already resumed their work at the first indication that the troglodyte was done with his presentation. They didn't hear the troglodyte slide in his first revision to border policy.

The troglodyte went back to his house and saw the day attendant in her booth, so assumed he would find his house empty as well. When he got to his place, he noticed that quite a few reflectors were missing from around his property but didn't worry much about it. After walking the walk around his property looking for damage, the troglodyte found some newspapers in his back yard. They were collected to give to the attendant. When the troglodyte opened the door to his house, he first heard the idle chat of the people inside before he saw them. There was a line for both the bathroom and the refrigerator, and were close to twenty people in his house.

The troglodyte asked what they all were doing there. They said they assumed the same as him, making use of the facilities. The troglodyte left the house without waiting in line for water. He grabbed one to the dismay of the people behind him and went to the toll booth. The attendant welcomed the troglodyte back, and told him all good things regarding the watching of his house. People had been tipping

her very graciously for allowing them to use it. The
troglodyte asked if his place was always that busy. She said
that the day previous had been the worst, once word had got
around about the rest stop. She figured today was shaping up
to beat that. The troglodyte asked if she needed any more
cases of water, or had to use the facilities herself. She said
that the lines had become too long. It was no longer any
more efficient than using the one available to toll booth and
public works employees. The troglodyte went back to his
house, and looked for the card of the business person
interested in estates. He found the buyer before he found the
card

③⓪

The troglodyte was in the basement when he bumped into the buyer, who was scribbling down notes and taking measurements. The buyer recognized the troglodyte as the man he had given a ride to previously, and asked if he was also there for the open house. The troglodyte told him that owning a home doesn't always go as planned, and had the paperwork to prove it. Which got the buyer's full attention. The buyer told the troglodyte all the things their clients usually like to hear before deciding to sell. He asked the troglodyte what it would take to get him out of the house and possibly into a new one. The troglodyte said it wouldn't take much, not even necessarily cash if the seller could get him away from this place to somewhere more secluded. The seller said that finding places like that was their specialty. The troglodyte may not even need to be patient if he moved fast.

The troglodyte asked for proof the agent was a specialist, and asked where the house was and what town it belonged to. Hearing that the property fell out of the jurisdiction of the surrounding towns because of some obscure zoning loophole, the troglodyte agreed immediately he would make the switch. Provided there were no close neighbors to speak of. The seller was just as eager to finalize a deal and invited the troglodyte to take a ride with them to the property, so the troglodyte could make a decision. The seller knew that the window for a sale was extremely short. Even in time consuming sales models such as buying a house. He suggested to the troglodyte anything he needed to sustain himself for a few hours should be brought. So they wouldn't have to stop along the way.

The drive took three hours on the main roads. About an hour and a half on some back roads. Two hours of walking. When the seller and the troglodyte arrived at the lot, the troglodyte was amazed at what good condition the house was in.He asked what had become of the previous owner. The seller said that the owner had inherited the house from a distant relative, but didn't last ten years and couldn't find it suitable for their lifestyle. The seller had been holding on to it for them, hoping that someone might be interested. The seller hadn't been able to convince any clients to make the trek to even check out the house, much less buy it, and asked the troglodyte what he thought. The troglodyte asked to see the inside. He was glad when he didn't find any furniture or any major appliances to speak of.

The seller said the water and electricity had been shut off.He could have them both on within the week. A home could be set up for the troglodyte, without him having to do anything other than lift a finger so that he could pen. The troglodyte asked the seller how much they would offer for his house. The seller said it would be an even trade, and asked the troglodyte where he saw himself in twelve years. The troglodyte's possessions would be moved from his place to the new one free of charge. The seller, having already seen the contents of the troglodyte's house, knew that it could all fit into one truck. It wouldn't be very costly to ship. The troglodyte asked what would become of his house. The seller said that for now it would remain as is. Once the area began to develop, it would most likely change to suit the environment.

The seller drove the troglodyte back to his place, to think on his decision, and would be back in no time to hear the answer. The troglodyte went into his house and drove all the people out when he began to work at his workbench. The smell of burning plastic became too much for them. When all the people had left, the troglodyte went around his house and locked all the doors and windows. Putting the key in his pocket after he had locked the front one from outside. He walked over to the attendant, hidden by the swarm of people entering the woods to look for their cars.

The troglodyte told the attendant about the offer on his house and asked what she would do if he were to sell. The attendant told him she would keep the water station open. She would probably still point customers in the house's direction if they needed the facilities, until she was no longer able to do so. She would also need to get the newspaper delivered to her place, but other than that, she supposed not much would change. The troglodyte and the attendant talked for a while longer, in between her serving customers, and parted after both gave each other words of encouragement and advice. The troglodyte didn't take any of the empty plastic back with him when he went to his house. Once inside, he again took inventory of his possessions and what he thought he would need to take with him.

The only essentials were his bed, the refrigerator and the workbench, but knew he planned on stuffing as much as possible into the truck when he moved. He had no way of calling the dealer from his house. He didn't want to borrow a phone in town just to rush back so he wouldn't miss a meeting. He ate a non perishable and went to sleep.

The next day the troglodyte woke to a knock on his door. When he opened it, he found a fresh crowd of anxious faces hoping to use his restroom. The troglodyte let them in as he went out, and borrowed a phone from someone walking in his direction. He got the dealer's card out of his pocket and called the number, telling them he was ready to do business. The dealer said that a truck would be at his place that day. The troglodyte could be sleeping in his new bed that night. The paperwork could be finalized shortly after. The troglodyte agreed to the truck arriving presently, and told the dealer he was ready to fall on his sword and sign the document.

The troglodyte went into town to close out any business he had to deal with, which primarily included canceling his mail delivery. He went to the barbershop, diner and gas station, to see how they were faring. He first went to the post office and broke the sticker on his locker to retrieve his mail log. He took it to the clerk, and told her that he no longer had any use for them. He would like all mail delivery to his location ceased. The clerk told the troglodyte that once he was in the system there was really only one way out. Even then, mail always had a forwarding address. The clerk asked the reason for the cancellation. He told her he was moving and didn't want to be contacted. The clerk offered to get in touch with the post office in the corresponding town, so that she may inform them of the troglodyte's request, but he thought that would be saying too much. He left the post office after telling the clerk to resume his mail as usual. He had faith that the postal worker would put any mail in the ditch once the chute was full, if they still chose to use that. If it had been the troglodyte's decision, he would've taken himself off of the postal worker's route because of the great job they had done. But since the clerk had refused to allow him to stop receiving mail, the worker would have to continue on with the frivolous task.

The troglodyte went to the diner next, and was seated once an empty spot had appeared at a booth. The troglodyte asked the waitress if she noticed anything different about him. She said he looked well rested, as if she didn't see what everyone else saw. The troglodyte said that like food tasting better, moving feels better when it is in front of you. She asked why the sudden change of scenery. The troglodyte said that he couldn't explain his reasoning but he just felt pulled in another direction. The waitress didn't take his order, but told him his meal was on the house. She went to the kitchen to put in her request. The troglodyte wasn't very excited about his last meal, but was still happy to have it, knowing he would soon be returning to a diet of non perishables. He wouldn't have to worry about variety or taste. When the waitress brought the troglodyte his food, he asked what it was. She told him it had been her favorite meal as a starving waitress. The chef had made it special for him.

He left a thoughtful tip when he was done eating and exited the restaurant, identifying all of the targeted demographics. From the diner the troglodyte walked the short distance to the barbershop, and received the welcome he would never be able to grow accustomed to. When the last hooray was hurrahed, the barber asked what could be done for him. The troglodyte told him he was thinking about growing his hair out and wanted some pointers on how to do so. The barber thought the troglodyte was being facetious, and told him to sit in the chair. When the troglodyte remained standing in the doorway, the barber suggested that he didn't look at his hair in the mirror every day. Other than that, the troglodyte should be alright. The troglodyte said they wouldn't be seeing much of him around the shop anymore. The patrons and barbers told him if he ever wanted a change of face, he knew where to look.

From there, he went to the gas station and saw a gang of smokers hanging around the pumps. The troglodyte asked the owner why they were smoking so close to the pumps. The owner said it was another tactic to draw in foot traffic. The troglodyte pointed out that the labels on the pumps had warnings that said explicitly not to smoke near them. The owner said that was just so the oil companies wouldn't get sued. The troglodyte asked the owner how they expected to not get sued if one of the pumps were to go up in flames. He said he would have more of a case than anyone injured. With the money he won from the suit he would be able to upgrade his lot, even if insurance wouldn't cover his negligence. The troglodyte bought a pack of cigarettes by overpaying for a bottle of water, and told the owner he was trying to kick the habit.

The troglodyte opened one of the cigarettes on the counter and rolled it back up after removing a good amount of tobacco. The troglodyte wondered out loud if the owner would be able to sell re-rolled cigarettes if they had just a percentage less of the tobacco that made it dangerous. The troglodyte left the owner with his train of thought, and didn't help any further with an enacting a plan.

The troglodyte took his pack of cigarettes across town to visit with the couple. When he got there the woman was at work. The man answered the door when he heard a knock and let the troglodyte inside to sit. The troglodyte said that the bicycle was working as expected and he gave thanks again for the present. He said that he was rescinding his invitation to the couple to visit because he was moving to a different location. They would no longer be able to find him. The man frowned when he heard the troglodyte's news. He did confess that he knew the day would come when the troglodyte would again be out of their lives.

The man thought out loud, listing things he could possibly gift for a farewell present but never found something worthy. If there was ever a possibility that there was a gift, he probably wouldn't have been thinking out loud, or at least wouldn't care about surprising. The troglodyte said that he did have something to give the man, and offered the pack of cigarettes. The troglodyte asked that the man share some with his partner, as it was for both of them. The troglodyte said that though it wasn't much, it was something they could remember him by until they finish the pack. By then the troglodyte would rather be forgotten. As the troglodyte walked away from the couple's house, the man stood at the front gate and called after him. He said the woman was on the phone and had something to say. The troglodyte, having already said his farewells, turned and looked at the man for about a minute. He then shook his head slowly from side to side, and headed back to the town's center.

The troglodyte went to the church and didn't have to
interrupt a service to be heard. The woman was in her office,
and told the troglodyte the door was open when she saw him
approach. The troglodyte said she shouldn't expect to see
him any time in the near future. She responded cryptically
that he shouldn't be so sure about that. She gave a short
discourse on humanity, it's struggles and unifications, and
pleaded that if the troglodyte were ever close by that he drop
in. Regardless of the stance he thought he was taking. The
troglodyte asked if any church would do. She supposed it
would. He thanked her and left.

The troglodyte went from the church to the bar and told
the barkeep he would have to find a way to keep the lights on
without him. The bar keep told the troglodyte that he had
been finding inspiration from some of the patrons at the bar.
Who had discovered wild marketing schemes that somehow
worked. Though the troglodyte had been a help, the barkeep
was sure he could manage to keep the lights on without him.
He told the troglodyte so, in order to assuage his worry. The
troglodyte asked the barkeep if the troupe was around. What
he and them had been working on. The man said they had
left town this past weekend, and were in search of fame and
fortune. The troglodyte was more excited than disappointed
with the news. He hoped that the troupe were able to find
both. The troglodyte ordered a beer for the road and went
back to his house to wait for the dealer.

When the troglodyte got back to his property he went to
the toll booth and tried to strike up a conversation with the
night attendant. The man didn't want to talk to the troglodyte
and told him the sooner he left the better. To which the
troglodyte said, it comes and goes, goes and comes, like a
snake, it isn't done. The attendant didn't want to partake in

the troglodyte's games, so shut the window and turned his back. The troglodyte got the message. He went to his house and unlocked the door. Not finding a note slid under the doorway when he entered, he looked all around the outside to see if the flipper had tried to leave a message. When he didn't find anything, he went back inside. He fell asleep as he waited.

The next morning he was woken to a knock on the door. The movers explained they were there to transport his belongings. The troglodyte showed them the workbench, refrigerator, bed and bike, saying those were the essentials and were to be given priority. The rest of the furniture was not as important. While the movers were carrying the troglodyte's possessions into the truck, the dealer walked into the house and said he was sorry that they didn't do this yesterday. They had been unable to find the troglodyte, and were unable to start the project. The troglodyte said that what mattered was that they were all here now. He followed the dealer to their car so that he could relocate.

The troglodyte remained silent while in the car, though his mind wasn't very occupied. The dealer told him of the school system in the surrounding towns and the recent boom to the local economy. More out of habit than for the troglodyte's benefit. When they got to the new house, the dealer brought the paperwork to a place where he could have the troglodyte sign. To finalize the transaction! The troglodyte said he preferred to wait until all of his stuff was delivered. The dealer showed him through the house again, and took him around the property so he could see where the line extended.

The moving truck pulled in as the dealer and the troglodyte were sitting near the front of the house. The two of them helped the movers get the troglodyte settled. When the movers had finished, and had stayed around the job site long enough to get a tip, they left. Leaving the troglodyte to deal with what was left. The troglodyte signed the form the dealer offered. Once he was assured the dealer would not contact him from now, until he was no longer in the house. Unless under extreme circumstances. The troglodyte said that if the dealer had to question if the circumstances were extreme enough, then they didn't know the definition of the word. If so, they should handle the matter on their own. The troglodyte walked the dealer to their car, and thanked them for helping in his smooth transition to home ownership. He watched the dealer drive off into the night on a path that was less traveled. Yet on it's way to becoming one not taken at all.

The troglodyte went into his house and sat at his workbench. There were tools but no materials. He felt content with his ordeal being over. Before going to bed he got a glass from a cabinet, and poured himself some water from the tap on the sink.

The next morning the troglodyte woke to a clean house and a property that was in order.